A KISS LIKE NO OTHER

Gerard's hand cupped Annette's chin. "You are a good woman, Miss Courtney. Probably too good for my London. But, yes, I would show my city to you."

Still holding her, he bent forward. His lips lightly brushed hers. At his soft touch, she felt his tentative question and stayed still in response.

She did not pull away, and he remained to kiss her longer and more fully. Annette's first surprise was how sweet his touch tasted. Her second was how tender he was.

His arms embraced her as her own experimentally crept up his chest. Beneath the rough tweed of his jacket, she could feel the strong breadth of his shoulders.

Praise for
The Spinster and the Wastrel

"Ms. Bergin's lavish attention to detail, sparkling dialogue, and thoroughly conflicted, endearingly flawed characters all mesh into a beautifully written 'keeper' that will leave readers yearning for more. Ms. Bergin's heroine, Annette Courtney, displays sly wit, real courage, and refreshingly demure sexiness, while her hero, Sir Gerard Montfort, comes across with more complexity and layers of character than some real-life men. You'll feel like these characters are your new best friends."

—*The Dallas Morning News*

The Spinster and the Wastrel

Louise Bergin

A SIGNET BOOK

SIGNET
Published by New American Library, a division of
Penguin Group (USA) Inc., 375 Hudson Street,
New York, New York 10014, U.S.A.
Penguin Books Ltd, 80 Strand,
London WC2R 0RL, England
Penguin Books Australia Ltd, 250 Camberwell Road,
Camberwell, Victoria 3124, Australia
Penguin Books Canada Ltd, 10 Alcorn Avenue,
Toronto, Ontario, Canada M4V 3B2
Penguin Books (N.Z.) Ltd, Cnr Rosedale and Airborne Roads,
Albany, Auckland 1310, New Zealand

Penguin Books Ltd, Registered Offices:
80 Strand, London WC2R 0RL, England

First published by Signet, an imprint of New American Library,
a division of Penguin Group (USA) Inc.

First Printing, January 2004
10 9 8 7 6 5 4 3 2 1

For Joe,
This first one is for you.
And for James, Stephen, and Laura,
because you always believed Mom could do it.

Chapter One

Miss Annette Courtney, spinster of Upper Brampton village in Wiltshire, sat patiently on her chair, waiting for Sir Nigel Montfort's will to be read. She did not mind the delay and watched as the other apparent beneficiaries settled themselves. For once, a roaring fire heated the grand drawing room at Hathaway Hall. She luxuriated in the opportunity to warm her bones, safe from the January winds lashing outside the windows. Since it would be most improper to stretch like a cat, Annette contented herself with curling and relaxing her formerly numbed fingers and toes. It had been a long, freezing wet walk from her cottage on the outskirts of the village to the manor house.

The extra chairs in the drawing room filled quickly as more men and women arrived. Hushed greetings were exchanged, as though they gathered in a church. Sir Nigel Montfort must not have been as much a miser in his will as he had been in real life. Most of the people Annette recognized were either from the village or servants of the estate. Along with the housekeeper, the cook, and the

Reverend Brown, she assumed she was to receive a small bequest.

She tried not to allow her hopes to rise too high, but any amount would be greatly appreciated. The collier, the butcher, and the merchant had all presented their bills to her for payment. The only question was, which one would no longer extend her any credit; he would be the one she paid. Prices had risen so much that she very much feared the income she relied on from her late mother's jointure would not support her throughout 1812, and the year had only begun.

Looking around, she saw that most of the chairs were filled and some of the people stood against the wall. The solicitor spread his papers out on a dark mahogany table set to one side of the hearth's fire. He stood so close to the blaze that his cravat drooped in the heat. She hoped the man would not take much longer to begin. The suspense filled her with anticipation.

Indeed, it surprised her that Sir Nigel had remembered her at all. The servants and the vicar were traditionally remembered in bequests, but Annette had never anticipated herself to be included. She would have thought the late baronet regarded her as a nuisance of the worst sort.

True, she had often plagued Sir Nigel for funds to assist the poor or the church's needs. Upon occasion she had even argued with him on behalf of his tenant farmers. Only after a great amount of pleading and persistence on her part, and continuous grumbling on his, would the old man dole out any of his money. Successful efforts left her departing Hathaway Hall with a drained feeling, as if her body had expended all its strength to pry free the few coins she clutched in her hands to help the poorest members of the village.

A sudden, deep laugh rang out over the subdued murmurings of the beneficiaries. It sounded louder than it should because everyone else was so quiet. Annette joined the others in seeking its source.

The man lounging in the best seat, a wing chair placed not too close, yet not too far from the hearth, paid no heed at becoming the center of remonstrative attention. He was dressed from head to toe in correct mourning black, which made his white linen gleam in the gray winter light of the room. His brown hair was combed into a fashionable style, yet its appearance was not so outrageous as to offend the country's sensibilities. The gold watch dangling from his fingers swung in time with his crossed leg. From his relaxed manner, Annette assumed he was the heir and new baronet, Sir Gerard Montfort. Village chatter had seethed with every tidbit of his arrival.

He spoke in a low tone to another man seated nearby. Gossip said a friend had accompanied the new heir. Annette ignored him in order to study the new baronet carefully. From the late Sir Nigel, she had heard much regarding his low opinion of the man who would succeed him. The old baronet often ranted about the extravagances and wastefulness of Gerard Montfort. Sir Nigel had greatly feared what would happen to his hoarded wealth when his nephew got his hands on the money.

"He's a wastrel!" Sir Nigel would thunder.

Annette had always agreed, even though she had never met the man. It was easier to listen to the lecture that accompanied any donation, rather than argue on behalf of someone she did not know. Now she wondered how much of the harangues she had endured were true. In her circumscribed life within the confines of Upper Brampton village, she had heard much about London wastrels, but she had never seen one.

If he was as negligent about money as his uncle claimed, perhaps she could convince him to support her plans for a school for the village and country children. Sir Nigel had always dismissed her project with a contemptuous snort and another lecture. He would never waste his money on a pack of dull brats, no matter how often Annette stated an education erased the stupidity. Even though she never managed to open the school, she tried to remain grateful for the donations she managed to wrest from the miser. Now she speculated at how successful she would be with the new baronet.

Sir Gerard looked rather striking. Despite the life of dissipation he was reputed to lead, no signs of it showed on his tall frame. His face had high cheekbones and the strong chin of a man of decisiveness. His jacket emphasized his broad shoulders, while his pantaloons encased the muscular legs of a man accustomed to hours on horseback. His appearance warred with his reputation. Not a young man, she decided. He was probably only a year or two older than her own age of thirty. She wondered why he had not married. Sir Nigel had also lectured her on the delinquent duties of his heir.

As if she had asked the question aloud, Sir Gerard suddenly looked at her. A grin spread across his face, making him appear almost lighthearted, which surely was an inappropriate action for the chief mourner. Resisting the urge to smile back, Annette pursed her lips. A wastrel with no sense of propriety, just as Sir Nigel had thundered.

Sir Gerard raised his eyebrows at her refusal of his friendly greeting. He shifted his body so his back was towards her and bent his head closer to his friend.

Annette sniffed, feeling guilty at her disdainful behavior. It was wrong of her to judge the man based upon the prejudicial rantings of his miserly uncle. When her late father was the vicar, she had heard many sermons, both in and out of church, regarding the judgment of one's fellow man. After all, now she would be coming to the new baronet whenever she needed a donation. Intending to make amends, she began to smile tentatively at the heir in case he glanced back towards her.

Then the solicitor cleared his throat.

Soft though the sound was, everyone immediately quieted as though a judge had banged a gavel. With avid expectation, they faced the man.

"Ladies and gentlemen, it is time to begin. I am Piers Keller, the late Sir Nigel Montfort's solicitor, and I appreciate your making the effort to be here for the reading of the will."

Polite murmurings answered him, but no one spoke aloud. Like Annette, they wanted to hear what they would receive.

With his wire-rimmed glasses perched firmly on the bridge of his nose, Piers Keller began. Annette could not understand all the whereases, wherefores, and other legal terms that filled the document, but she paid close attention when the list of individual bequests started.

Sir Nigel was surprisingly generous to his servants. Even his tenants received a few coins back. When the solicitor announced the munificent amount intended for the church, a surprised gasp echoed around the room. Plainly, after death, Sir Nigel's reputation was going to be brightly burnished in the village.

From the corner of her eye, Annette noticed that Sir Gerard Montfort no longer lounged on his chair. Instead, he sat bolt upright, a frown creasing his face. The prospect of so much wealth leaving his grasp through bequests obviously dismayed him. With an inward sigh, Annette feared she would be dealing with another miser in Upper Brampton village.

The solicitor had reached the end of the list of bequests without mentioning her name. He paused to take a breath. Excitement quivered throughout the room, as if it were a tangible part of the beneficiaries. Annette wondered if her name had been overlooked in the reading; she was certain she would have heard if it had been mentioned.

"To my nephew, Gerard Montfort, the new Baronet Westcourt, I leave all the entailed property including the title and the estate Hathaway Hall with its attached lands and house. All unentailed property and the balance of my wealth, I leave to Miss Annette Courtney, spinster of Upper Brampton village."

For an instant, shocked silence hung in the air, then a reflexive gasp filled the drawing room. All eyes turned to stare at Annette. She stared back in disbelief. The room began to swim before her eyes. A loud roaring filled her ears, and she wondered if she was going deaf. Certainly she could not have heard what she thought she had heard.

A sudden shout broke the incredulous spell. "No! I don't believe it!" Sir Gerard Montfort sprang to his feet and strode over to snatch the will from the solicitor's hands. "My uncle would never do such a thing to me."

Piers Keller drew himself up to his full height, but he was still five inches below the angry heir. "I assure you, this is what Sir Nigel wished."

Sir Gerard stared at the paper. "It cannot be. Just the lands and the title? Only what the entail required him to bestow? None of the money?"

"Yes, sir."

"Why?"

The solicitor cleared his throat and carefully took the will back into his hands. "I believe he did not trust you with his money."

"But I am his nephew. To whom else should it go?"

"Sir Nigel selected Miss Courtney."

"And just who *is* this Miss Courtney?" Sir Gerard sneered.

Annette stood on legs that wobbled beneath her skirts. "I am."

Aware of everyone's stares, she approached the table. Sir Gerard cast her a contemptuous look. Suddenly Annette was very conscious of her serviceable brown woolen dress and the severity of her hairstyle. To his London eyes, she probably appeared like a maidservant, instead of the daughter of the deceased vicar.

"Quite the adventuress, aren't you, Miss Courtney? You obviously possess the talent necessary to swindle my uncle's money from him."

His gibe stung Annette. "This is just as much a surprise to me as it is to you."

"It is a surprise to *me*," he acknowledged with his dark eyes narrowed in suspicion.

Her ire began to stir within her. After all, she had withstood his uncle. The nephew was not going to browbeat her. Only by recalling how much of a jolt the news was could she rein in her tongue. With an effort, she turned to the solicitor. "What does that last part of the will mean?"

"It means you are a very rich woman," Keller replied. "Once all the beneficiaries have been paid, you receive the remainder of the money. The only things Sir Nigel could not give you were the lands and the title, which are entailed. He only had a life interest in them, the same as Sir Gerard has now."

"But I need the money to go with it!" the baronet exclaimed. "This will cannot stand. It is totally ridiculous!"

The solicitor stiffened with affront. "I assure you that Sir Nigel was of sound mind when he outlined his wishes to me."

"Then I want you to break it." Menace threatened behind Sir Gerard's order.

"I cannot do that."

"Why not?"

"I was the one who drew up this will for Sir Nigel. It is legal in every respect."

Sir Gerard nearly shouted with anger. "You drew up this monstrous display of injustice? What type of solicitor goes against all common decency in such a way?"

The man tried to soothe the angry baronet. "I did my best to point out the injustice in his plans, but Sir Nigel would not listen. He was determined not to give you a farthing more than he must. I did do my best, sir."

"Your best is obviously not competent enough for me. I will break this will."

"You can try." Annette heard the tartness in the solicitor's voice. "If you have the money, you can try anything, but I warn you. This will *is* sound. It will stand."

Sir Gerard flung up his hands and turned to face the beneficiaries. "I want you out of my house now. After all, Hathaway Hall is still mine, is it not?"

Subdued, Keller replied, "Of course it is, sir."

Grumbling greeted Sir Gerard's order. As people pushed back their chairs and stood, Annette knew they were disappointed to be sent home without the traditional reception after the reading of the will. She recognized that many of the villagers were dressed in their Sunday best clothes in honor of the trip to Hathaway Hall. Sending them away so abruptly would not endear the new baronet to them. Memories lasted a long time in the country. Living in London, he could not be expected to know that. Since she was used to defending the villagers' interests, it was her duty to inform him, no matter how much she dreaded his anger.

She cleared her throat. "Sir Gerard, I believe the people expected to be offered something to eat. After the reading, a small reception is a common practice around here."

He stared at her in disbelief, his brown eyes as hard as the oak trees that lined his lands. "First you take my money, and now you expect me to feed you?"

"The money was not yours," she pointed out. "It belonged to Sir Nigel to do what he wished with it." Annette had paid close attention to the bitter exchange between the baronet and the solicitor. She had not yet grasped the extent of her new riches, but she knew she was a wealthy woman. "Sir, you can be gracious. After all, these people will be your neighbors and tenants for as long as you are at Hathaway Hall."

He shot a bitter glare at her. "That's correct. I only have a *life* interest in it."

He flung himself around to face the beneficiaries who had stood but had made no further move to leave while such dramatics played before them. "Very well. You may eat. The meal is laid in the dining room." He turned back to Annette. "Since the food is not entailed, I assume it is at *your* expense they will be eating. You can entertain them. I am going to my room, where I expect to enjoy a private bottle of brandy—if you don't begrudge it, Miss Courtney."

"Of course, I do not," she answered tartly. "It is yours."

"I am not sure what is mine anymore." He spun on his heel to leave and then faced her once more. "Miss Courtney, don't get too comfortable with my money and spend it all. I will get it back. I promise you that."

He marched from the drawing room, leaving the door wide open behind him. His friend followed him out. In the taut silence that ensued, Annette could hear Sir Gerard stamp up the stairs. When the sound of a distant door crashing reached the drawing room, it acted like a plug yanked free from a drain. A torrent of chatter arose as everyone spoke at once, offering an opinion about what had occurred.

Annette faced the solicitor and smiled weakly. "Mr. Keller, could you explain what has happened? What does this will mean?"

Slamming the door behind himself may have been a childish act, but Sir Gerard Montfort found satisfaction in hearing it crash. At least something obeyed him. He strode over to the brandy decanter the butler kept filled in the master suite.

After splashing some of the amber liquid into a crystal glass, he turned to survey his room. His uncle's servants had kept it clean. No smell of damp hung in the air, but the furnishings represented an era fashionable before Sir Gerard's birth. The once rich yellow bed hangings were faded with age, and the bed itself was of an oppressive dark wood. The chair by the fire showed a newer fabric pattern, probably because the original had worn out past mending. Sir Nigel had disliked spending a farthing on anything other than what was strictly necessary for his personal comfort. Against one wall, an armoire squatted, so small that not even half of Sir Gerard's wardrobe would fit into it. He would have to replace it. Actually, he intended to replace all of the furniture, preferring the more delicate lines now in style.

Yet, his plans took money. He gave a muffled oath. He had none. The furniture might not even be his to change. Everything depended upon what the entail included. Indeed, the brandy he now held in his hand was probably not his, since it was not likely to be included in the entail. All of it belonged to that woman.

When he had noticed her studying him, he had assumed her to be one of his uncle's pensioners who worried about her future. His smile had meant to reassure her, but she had turned away. From shyness he had thought! Intrigued by the youth of this "charity case," he had intended to become better acquainted after the reading of the will.

Well, his eyes had been opened. She was no poor pensioner, but an adventuress. She stole his money, but she would not keep it. She probably would have taken his title, too, if she could have.

Like his uncle, she apparently judged him of little account. Someone she could rob with impunity. His uncle had named him a wastrel and worthless, but this time he would prove the insults wrong.

At last he was the fifth Baronet Westcourt. He would get the money back and take his rightful place at the head of society. A man others respected.

With a proud sneer, he toasted himself and drank some of the brandy. It burned going down his throat, although the vintage was a good one. He could not fault his uncle's concern for his personal comfort.

A knock sounded on the door, and he growled, "Come in."

Robert Linton ambled in. His closest friend had accompanied him on the trip from London to support him through the bereavement process. Average in height, Linton wore his brown hair in a simple fashion and dressed in black mourning clothes as a sign of respect—respect Sir Gerard no longer felt his uncle deserved. He saw the concern in Linton's hazel eyes and turned away to conceal his own emotions. The brandy sloshing in his glass betrayed his shaking hands. The precipice of social disaster loomed too close.

"Care for a drink?" Sir Gerard asked, indicating the decanter on the table. "After hearing that will, I needed one."

Linton nodded his agreement as he poured himself a glass. After sipping it, he asked, "What are you going to do now?"

"I have to break the will. I must get that money."

His friend compressed his lips. "It will not be easy."

"Do I have a choice?"

Linton knew the true state of his circumstances. "Breaking a will takes time," he said. "You do not have much of it."

"I know." Sir Gerard swirled his brandy. "My gambling debts must be settled soon, or else every door in London will be closed against me. I will be an outcast. I could not bear that." Recalling Linton's financial problems, he cast an apologetic glance at him. "I regret I cannot help you out of your difficulties as I had planned."

The other man shrugged. "No matter. The money-lender will just have to be patient a bit longer."

Sir Gerard frowned. Linton had introduced him to that same money-lender where he borrowed a sum that now seemed to be a staggering amount. "I dislike the interest mounting up while he waits. I did not expect to have to pay him very much when I gave him my note."

"Perhaps you celebrated your elevation to the title a little too soon."

Sir Gerard cast his friend a sour look. "As I recall, you were right there alongside me."

A reminiscent smile flitted across Linton's face. "It was certainly dashed good fun. Who knew what evil your uncle had plotted? To give you the title, but not the means to support it." He shook his head in disbelief.

Sir Gerard strolled over to the fire and leaned against the mantel. "Perhaps it was not all my uncle's fault. Perhaps an adventuress lurks beneath the façade of a spinster. Did you get a look at her? I knew my uncle to be eccentric, but not that he was a fool, too."

"She does not look like the typical adventuress," Linton agreed. "Too tall and skinny. And the way she dressed! Her clothes looked like rags hanging on a pole." He shuddered at the picture.

"We plainly underestimate her charms or her abilities, since she was able to worm her way into my uncle's affections. I was never able to do it, even though I was his heir." He took another swallow of his drink, but this time the taste seemed as bitter as his memories. "She is obviously a dangerous woman, but she will discover I can be an equally dangerous opponent. This is one contest I do not intend to lose."

Chapter Two

"*You* inherited all the money!" Lucille Downes's squeal of surprise sounded just like that of the pigs her farmer husband used to raise. In her late forties, her face was as round as her body, which she draped with ruffles and furbelows. The circle of her mouth copied her wide brown eyes as the woman stared at Annette. The shock registered on her face echoed the reverberations the new heiress still felt within herself.

"I could not believe it, either," Annette told her companion.

The two women were seated in the genteelly furnished drawing room of the cottage they shared. Despite the small fire flickering in the grate, the room remained chilled, and they sought both warmth and sustenance from their tea.

After the vicar had passed away, Annette and her invalid mother moved from the church manse, but the new cottage's rent was a heavy expense. When Lucille was widowed, she, too, was required to move. Without a son to inherit the farm's tenancy and no living daughter obliged to care for her surviving parent, Lucille was in desperate straits. She faced the dreaded parish poorhouse. When Annette suggested they share the cottage's expenses and care of Mrs. Courtney, Lucille welcomed the opportunity.

Annette had overheard her neighbors' puzzled speculation about the success of two such disparate women living in the same house. She knew she was renowned in Upper Brampton village for her managing ways. She met every one of life's hurdles with squared shoulders and a no-nonsense approach, while Lucille bowed before life's difficulties with a quiet resignation. Even though Annette could not understand her companion's approach, she had always been grateful for the extra care her invalid mother had received from the other lady. No one denied Lucille's generous heart.

Now hope warred with disbelief in the widow's brown, puppylike eyes. "This isn't a joke, is it?"

"I could not believe it myself, at first, but it is true," Annette assured her. "The solicitor wants to meet with me tomorrow to sign the papers."

"How much money is there? There must be pots of it. Old Sir Nigel was such a miser."

"That will be one of my questions to Mr. Keller."

Lucille's sigh of satisfaction drew from deep within. "To think you will never have to worry about the tradesmen again!"

"You're right!" At the realization, the great burden of anxiety she had carried for so long slipped from Annette's shoulders with almost a physical lightening. A buoyant feeling of freedom now filled her.

She looked around the small drawing room, where they worked to keep up the appearance of gentility. The dark wood furniture remained dust free because their labor was free. Expense forced them to do the light housekeeping, while relying on an intermittent maid to do the heavy work. Beautiful embroidery from the needle of her late mother adorned the seat covers. Although an invalid for many years before her death, Mrs. Courtney had left behind a colorful legacy of fabric that still surrounded her daughter.

The small fire seemed more for show and to provide light in the winter afternoon gloom than for warmth. Setting down her teacup, Annette rubbed her hands, still chilled from the walk home. She stood, took some wood from the box, and built up the flame until it roared. Ashes swirled from her vigorous efforts, and she coughed as one lodged in her throat.

"What are you doing?" Lucille asked. "Why are you making the fire so high?"

"Starting as of now, we never have to be cold again." Annette held her hands out to the blaze, feeling its heat clear to her bones. She shivered with delight and turned back to her friend. "How wonderful it will be to never fear the collier, or the butcher, or the apothecary, or anyone else again."

Lucille clapped her hands at the prospect. "Yes! Oh, Annette, what are you going to do with all that money?"

"Why, I had not considered it." She blinked as she tried to order her thoughts. "Most important, of course, is to pay off all the tradesmen's bills."

"Pooh! Why must you always be so practical! This is your chance to gain what you have always wanted. Picture something more—your heart's deepest desire."

"Paying off the tradesmen *is* one of my deepest desires." Yet a picture of a village school sprang into her mind. At Lucille's frown, Annette added, "What did you have in mind?"

The other woman tittered. "*My* wishes are of no concern because it is not my money."

Uncertain, Annette slowly sat on her chair. For one of the few times in her life, she was confused. All of her upbringing had taught her to stretch a penny, not manage pounds. "You are my dearest friend. Certainly your wishes are my concern. I do not know what to do, and I need your help."

"Help you spend the money?" Lucille exclaimed. "Gladly! Have you never wanted to travel? Go to London? Buy new dresses?" She twitched her skirt with a disdainful air and shook her head at her friend's dress. "We can begin with that right now."

The prospect tempted Annette, but she continued to hesitate. "It sounds so frivolous to spend the money that way."

"You have not had enough frivolity in your life to enable you to enjoy it when the opportunity appears," Lucille replied tartly. "This is your chance."

"I thought opening a school for the local children would be a more worthy cause."

Lucille threw up her hands. "Why must you only spend the money on some type of charity? If you want a worthy cause, use it to find yourself a husband."

"Buy one, you mean."

The other woman defiantly met Annette's gaze. "Why not? You are thirty years of age."

"Yes, and passed the age of marrying." Annette picked up her teacup and sipped from it. The tea was cold, just like her prospects for falling in love and marrying.

The widow sighed. When she spoke again, her tone had lost its stridency. "You did your duty when you cared for your mother throughout the years of your maidenhood.

Perhaps this inheritance is God's way of rewarding you so
you can still have a husband and children."

Annette tried to smile. Even more than a school, children were her deepest desire. "Who would want me now?
When I was younger, I was too plain and dowerless to attract any man willing to take on the additional duty of my
mother's care. Now I do not want a man who only sees the
money. I want love and will not settle for less."

"You could pretend," the other woman muttered into
her teacup.

Annette pretended not to hear her. As she contemplated
her inheritance, a small bit of guilt gnawed at her conscience. Her good fortune resulted from another's loss. "I
thought the money should have gone to Sir Gerard Montfort."

"The new baronet?" When Annette nodded, Lucille
continued, "It is plain that old Sir Nigel did not share your
opinion of his heir. You said he only referred to his nephew
as 'that wastrel.' Was the man at the reading?"

"Yes," Annette answered. "And very angry, too."

"No surprise there," Lucille commented. "What was he
like?"

Unexpectedly, the picture of Sir Gerard that sprang into
Annette's mind was far more complete than she had anticipated. His image was as sharp as if it was painted by a
master artist, so completely did she recall details she had
not remembered noticing. For one of the few times in her
life, she had been forced to look up to speak to a man. Although no smile had charmed his face, his chin had been
strong and his brown eyes remarkably clear. His figure remained trim, despite his reputation. Although his life was
certainly one of dissipation, no signs of it yet marked him.
The discrepancy bothered her.

She tried to explain the mystery to Lucille. "He was not what I had expected for someone known to be a wastrel."

"I have never seen a wastrel."

"Neither have I, but he looked far better than I would have thought one did."

Lucille brightened. "Is he handsome?"

Resting her chin on her hand, Annette considered. "Handsome seems the wrong word. He was noticeable. Although he ignored everyone else in the drawing room, we were aware of his presence."

"Naturally, since he is a new face in the area. I wonder if he will attend any of the local Assemblies."

"We are likely too provincial for him. Remember, he is used to London society."

"Pooh! With your money, you can now afford an entrée into society." She snuggled deeper into her chair and hugged her wool shawl closer as she contemplated the future.

Unwilling to disillusion her friend, Annette's answer was only a noncommittal, "Perhaps."

She believed it took more than money to enter the *ton*. As the daughter of the late vicar, Annette would not be turned away from local affairs, and Lucille would be accepted as her companion. Yet making a splash in society had never been her dream. She wanted a family, but now that she firmly sat on the shelf, she was doomed to never have little ones of her own. This inheritance could not change the past.

The money could not fulfill her deepest wish, but perhaps she could use it to help others. In gratitude for nursing her mother, Annette would never allow Lucille to worry ever again. When her father was the vicar, she had assisted him with the relief of the poor. She was well aware of the suffering within the village of Upper Brampton. Her life had been spent in service to others. She would continue along that path, but now she no longer needed to beg for the coins.

A smile tugged at her lips. Tomorrow she would discuss the possibilities for Lucille's future and a village school with Mr. Keller. She would hire the solicitor to help her with her plans. Sir Gerard Montfort might dislike her gaining his inheritance, but Annette no longer had to worry about pleasing the Baronet Westcourt. It was a very agreeable feeling.

As the newest Baronet Westcourt, Sir Gerard did not think he was being accorded the respect due his rank. After the initial cordial greeting, Piers Keller's face had smoothed into a blank gaze. *Even the wrinkles seemed to disappear*, Sir Gerard thought irritably. Nothing remained to give away the solicitor's thoughts. The stuffy smell of leather books permeated the office, crowded with piles of papers. Although Sir Gerard was used to hunching over a green baize table to gamble, he felt hemmed in. Yet he would not allow such discomfort to interfere with his mission. He intended to get his money back.

Piers Keller made a steeple of his hands, but Sir Gerard met the man's assessment with a level stare of his own. He would not be intimidated by such manners.

"You wish to break the will?" the solicitor asked.

Sir Gerard determined there would be no misunderstanding. "Yes. The money belongs to me and to the estate. It was wrong of my uncle to separate the two. I regard it as proof that his mind was unhinged."

The other man tapped his fingers together. "Sir Nigel

had full use of his mental faculties when he ordered the conditions of the will."

Sir Gerard snorted. "I take leave to doubt that. Look at the results. He must have been mad."

More finger-tapping. "You will find it a difficult proposition to have him declared thus. Until the day of his heart seizure, Sir Nigel remained as alert as any other man. Indeed, he was sharper than most." Keller leaned forward. "Since you were in London, how do you propose to prove your assertion? All the witnesses are here where Sir Nigel lived and where you did not visit."

In frustration, Sir Gerard slammed his fist on the desk, making the quill pens bounce. "You are a solicitor. Certainly I can hire you to overturn the will."

Mild interest appeared on the other man's face. "Do you have the funds to pursue such a course? For I believe it is my duty to warn you the case will be both lengthy and expensive."

Time and money. The two things he could not afford now. Back in London, gambling debts howled to be paid, and that money-lender would not wait forever.

At first his uncle's death had appeared to be a fortuitous blessing, now he faced social ruin if he did not honor his notes. Still the solicitor's attention boded well for his hopes.

He settled back in his chair as hope began to stir within him. "Why should it be so difficult and costly to get the money back? After all, Miss Courtney appears to be only a poor spinster. If I offered her a settlement to avoid the legal hassles, I should think she would be quite happy to return the funds."

"The will is a solid document, designed to withstand challenges."

Sir Gerard permitted himself a smile. "It can still be overturned. If you are not capable of undertaking the task, I will hire someone who is. London has many capable lawyers."

The solicitor stiffened. "*I* wrote that will, and it will not be overturned. Not even if you bring your hired legal experts from London. You may regard my abilities as only suitable for the country, but the law rules even in the farthest corners of England. Even in Upper Brampton village."

"That will is a miscarriage of justice!"

Keller stood and frowned. "You will not break this will. No matter how hard you try. It is as solid as the rocks in the ground. Should Miss Courtney ask, my advice will be to refuse any of your *settlements*. They were not the intentions of Sir Nigel. He was my client for many years, and I will not disobey his wishes."

Sir Gerard heard the conviction in the man's voice and believed it. He could always spend the resources of time and money he did not possess, but the end result would still be his defeat. Although he enjoyed gambling, he knew better than to place his stake against a certain outcome.

The next minutes passed in a blur. Somehow he managed to stand and say all the correct things as he took his farewell of the stiffly polite solicitor, but all he could envision was the social abyss that yawned before him. Nothing, it seemed, could save him.

When Sir Gerard opened the door to exit the office, he met the solicitor's next client. The woman waiting there was now the bane of his existence. Although he glowered at her, Miss Annette Courtney's smile of greeting lit up her rather plain face, and he felt ashamed of his rudeness. It was definitely not proper *ton* to display one's emotions.

In an effort to recover his manners, he bowed to her. "Good afternoon, Miss Courtney. I trust you are well."

"Thank you, sir, I am." Her voice was crisp with each syllable clearly enunciated. There would be no misunderstanding in her speech.

After the stuffy atmosphere of the office, her brisk manner cut through the fog surrounding him like a brilliant lantern. He peered more closely at her and caught a whiff of her perfume. It was a light scent, which seemed to be at odds with the serviceable dark dress she wore and the practical bonnet. No fashionable woman of his acquaintance would be caught dead in such a contraption. The contradiction between the sweetness of the violet perfume and the severe clothes puzzled him.

To detain her from entering the office, he asked, "Are you here to consult with Mr. Keller?"

"Yes. There are papers I need to sign and plans I wish to discuss."

With his money, but he noticed she did not emphasize the fact. His smile became stiff. He did not begrudge her a new wardrobe, at a modest cost, of course. It was those unspoken "plans" that filled him with dread. Despite the solicitor's warning, Sir Gerard determined he would offer a settlement to this woman, before she wasted his inheritance.

"I have a proposal to place before you," he said.

Her eyes widened in shock. "A proposal?"

Damn! An unfortunate choice of words. Now the adventuress probably anticipated acquiring his title along with his wealth.

"No, not quite a proposal . . ." He started to clarify his meaning and then paused. Perhaps the title would lure her into listening to him. Once the actual negotiating over the settlement commenced, certainly her true nature would be revealed. The difficulty would be getting her to agree to only a portion of the money when she now possessed all of it.

Sir Gerard swallowed and began again. "Let us say, an idea I think you will find to be of interest."

"Indeed, sir, you intrigue me greatly."

I will wager I do interest you, he thought cynically. In the dim lighting, he could not be certain, but he assumed there was a mercenary gleam of interest in her eyes. He stepped forward to look more closely and again caught a whiff of violets.

"Why wait, then? Let me call on you now to discuss my idea." He extended his arm, prepared to escort her from this office.

The solicitor cleared his throat. Sir Gerard had forgotten the man remained in the room.

"Miss Courtney," Keller said, "acting as your representative, I would advise you not to listen to the baronet. He can be a charmingly persuasive man."

She dropped the hand she had placed on Sir Gerard's arm. "Forgive me, I nearly forgot I have an appointment to see Mr. Keller."

An oath struggled for expression within Sir Gerard, but he managed to maintain a polite smile. "Of course, you must keep your commitments." He understood commitments. They were something he was striving to fulfill with regard to his debts.

"I endeavor to be punctual," she said in a prim tone.

"Another time, then, I look forward to being the appointment you keep. Will you be punctual with me?" From his habit of dealing with women, he winked at her.

She drew her breath in sharply at his flirtatious gesture,

and a pleased feeling filled him. He would bet she had not been the recipient of much coquetry, not and yet remain a spinster. At that instant a suggestion sprang into his mind. He would use his charm to regain his money. It had provided for him in the past. It could do the same now.

"But . . . but of course," she replied, flustered. "Punctuality is a virtue."

"I am certain you are always virtuous." The words left a sour taste in his mouth. It was such self-righteously virtuous people like his uncle who judged him without a hearing.

"No one can be virtuous without God's help."

If her eyes had been cast down, he would have suspected her of false meekness, but she met his gaze directly. Pinned by the surety in her clear brown eyes, it was his turn to feel flustered. "Er, yes, of course. You will not forget I intend to call on you to discuss my . . . my proposal?"

"I will not forget," she promised.

He believed her, for she was the type of woman who kept her word. Although unable to prevent her meeting with the solicitor, he thought he might still salvage something from this mess.

"Until then." Sir Gerard bowed his farewell.

When he straightened up, he caught the trace of that elusive violet perfume scenting the air. It was so out of place in the office that he nearly sniffed like a hunting dog. Maintaining his composure, he retrieved his hat and gloves from the clerk and stepped outside. The cold air stung his cheeks, clearing the stuffiness of the solicitor's rooms from his mind. Pulling his hat lower on his head, he welcomed the chill because it served to sharpen his wits. He would need every bit of cleverness he possessed to wheedle his money free from this adventuress.

Slowing his stroll to the livery, he was no longer certain his charm would work. The clarity of her gaze as it met his shook him deeply. He continued to name her an adventuress, but she was unlike the London ladies with whom he was familiar. They simpered at his coquetry and responded with outrageous quips of their own.

At the reading, he had judged Annette Courtney plain. How had he overlooked the strength and determination that were obviously so much a part of her character? From the way she held her shoulders straight, not hiding her tall height, to the way she faced him directly, even when his words flustered her, she was different. The discrepancy bothered him. It could be harder than he had anticipated retrieving his money.

He collected his beloved horse, Silver Shadow, from the stables. He rubbed the gray stallion's nose and listened to his nickers of welcome. Animals never judged him. They gave their loyalty without question.

"Did they treat you royally?" he asked the horse.

The animal nudged him back playfully. When Sir Gerard mounted and headed home, his problems still weighed on his mind, but the feel of the strongly muscled horse beneath him lessened those worries.

He exulted in the way they moved together down the wet, snowy lanes. He did not race because Silver Shadow was too precious to risk, yet he rejoiced at the sting of the wind against his face and the sound of his horse's hooves echoing in the winter quiet. He was still master here.

Amazingly, even though it was January, a whiff of springtime violets seemed to hang in the air.

Chapter Three

Annette had expected there would be piles of paperwork associated with her inheritance, but she had not
anticipated the amount of detail her new wealth required.
It overwhelmed her, forcing her meeting with Sir Gerard
from the center of her attention. She had signed her name
so often that her pen needed re-sharpening.

Despite having lived in Upper Brampton all of her life,
she discovered how little she knew of the village's financial underpinnings. Naturally, the entailed farms were not
a part of her inheritance, but she could claim ownership to
several prime parcels of pastureland, including the lush
Green Meadow. She also held an interest in several shops,
which the solicitor assured her would provide her with a
steady income. The sum he quoted made her wonder how
the merchants earned any profit.

"However," Piers Keller continued with his list, only
this time Annette noticed an almost pained frown on his
face, "you will not be receiving anything from the old
warehouse. Ever since that new storage place opened
down south, the farmers have preferred to take their crops
over there."

"You mean that great empty building behind the general store is mine, too?" Annette had always assumed it belonged to the shopkeeper.

Keller nodded. "Yes, Sir Nigel accepted it in place of a defaulted loan, but he never kept it up. Now the repairs would be so expensive, the place could never turn a profit. You might as well let it fall down on its own."

"Falling down was not the fate I was considering," she said. Her dream of a village school leapt fully formed into her mind. She could see the children eagerly seated in rows on their benches as they learned. Perhaps now she could see those children gathered in reality.

She leaned forward to mention the school when she realized the solicitor had continued with his enumeration of her possessions.

"There is quite a bit of money tied up in securities. I would not recommend that you sell them, because they are currently giving a solid yield of two percent." He wagged his finger at her. "You never want to make the mistake of selling your capital. Live within your means."

"I certainly intend to do so," she replied, wondering how he thought she had managed before on a far littler income. "What will the amount of interest be?"

He harrumphed and stared at her sternly. "You should receive about one thousand pounds annually. I can advance you fifty pounds today. You will receive the remainder once the bank is instructed that you are the new owner."

"A thousand pounds!" Annette echoed weakly. "With fifty for today!"

She was grateful she was sitting down because the news caused black spots to swim before her eyes. The smell of book leather, paper, and candle wax overwhelmed her as her sight faded. She had never had much use for women who fainted, but for the first time in her life, a swoon was possible.

"Miss Courtney! Are you all right?"

With a start, Annette realized she had slumped in her chair. The solicitor stood beside her. He patted her wrists, his brow twisted with concern.

"May I get you something? Water?" He hesitated. "Or would you prefer some ratafia?"

Annette smiled slightly. Her mind clearing, she doubted such a female drink would be available in such a masculine enclave as a solicitor's office. "You actually have some ratafia here?"

He shook his head. "I can send my clerk out for it, if you wish."

"What a difficult client you must anticipate me to be." She straightened up and smoothed her skirt. "A glass of water will suffice."

When it had been procured, Annette once again turned her attention to the wealth they were discussing. Now that she knew how much of a miser Sir Nigel had been, she wondered at the hardness of his heart and regretted she had not convinced him to further help the unfortunate. The small donations she had wrested from him had been dearly won. At least she would never be in the position of begging from his nephew.

"Mr. Keller, why did Sir Nigel leave his money to me? Should it not have gone to Sir Gerard?"

The solicitor steepled his fingers and looked over them at her. "Sir Nigel spent his life acquiring his wealth and made his investments carefully. He respected money."

Annette thought he had worshiped it, but she did not interrupt.

"The old baronet did not want his life's work to be wasted. He wanted it to be conserved and knew you would care for it wisely."

"I am not a miser," she burst out. "He only knew me because I hounded him for donations—meager though they were."

Keller nodded. "True, but the money he gave you was well spent. You were reliable, while his nephew's reputation proved otherwise."

Annette knew she had used Sir Nigel's donations prudently. Was her wise use of his charity the reason she had inherited? Her biblical training had taught her that if a man could be trusted in small things, he could be trusted in larger.

"Perhaps Sir Gerard's reputation was exaggerated or inaccurate," she suggested. The amount of money was so large she feared an injustice might have been done.

"I doubt it." The man's tone was as dry as the paper filling his office. "Sir Nigel often received stories from London about his nephew's attendance at society parties where gambling occurred." He nodded significantly at her. "When tasked with it, Sir Gerard only asked for a loan to live on. The old baronet knew better than to finance such a risky proposition. He never even gave his nephew an allowance. That man earned his reputation as a wastrel."

Annette's eyes widened at the revelation. "No allowance? How did Sir Gerard survive?"

Shrugging, Keller replied, "Apparently by his wits. Don't waste your sympathy on him. He knows how to watch out for himself. He has done it all of his life."

It amazed her that Sir Gerard had looked so much like a gentleman, considering his lack of income. A member of the *ton* would never stoop to work to support himself, so successful gambling must be the answer. Yet it bothered her that she was the recipient of the wealth, though she could understand Sir Nigel's thinking. She would not want the money wasted on gambling either. She had other, better, plans for it.

The solicitor cleared his throat. "Now that we have gone over your inheritance, do you have any immediate plans for it?"

Annette nodded her head briskly and inched her chair closer to his desk. "Yes, I do. I will take that fifty pounds you mentioned and use it to pay off some of my bills. Then I want to take a closer look at that warehouse. I think it would be the perfect site for my school."

Keller blinked. "School? What school?"

"I have long wanted the children of Upper Brampton and the surrounding farms to attend a school, but the families are too poor to pay for one." Enthusiasm filled Annette. The reality of her dream was taking shape. Her words tumbled over each other as she poured out the wish of her heart. "I could never collect enough donations to start one of my own. There were always more pressing needs. Now I can use that old warehouse. I have enough money to both help the unfortunate in the village and teach their children. This is a wonderful opportunity."

The solicitor held up his hands in an effort to slow the onslaught. "Have you given this matter enough thought, Miss Courtney? You only learned the extent of your holdings today."

"True, but I have wanted to open a school for so long." She smiled with excitement. "I even requested Mr. Patterson donate the use of his warehouse. Of course, when he refused me, I did not know that it no longer belonged to him."

"He was likely ashamed to tell you about his defaulted loan," Keller commented.

"Very possible," Annette agreed, but she was more interested in her future plans than what had happened in the past. "The first thing to do is have the warehouse inspected and make any necessary repairs. I also must alert the neighbors the school will soon be opening."

The solicitor cleared his throat. "There are some questions you must consider before opening the school, such as who will be the teacher? What will be taught? Who will be the students and how much will you charge them?"

Annette laughed. "Don't worry so. I have the answers. I will be the teacher, and the children will learn reading, arithmetic, and their Bible. I already told you the students will be from the village."

"The village children!" From the shock on his face, he plainly had not heard her before. He drummed his fingers on the desktop. "When you said a school, I assumed you meant for young ladies. Why would you want to teach the locals? An education would be cruel. It will only give them ideas above their station that can never be fulfilled."

An iron bar seemed to slide along Annette's back, and she straightened up in her chair. The excitement vanished from her voice when she answered. Only the crisp tones she habitually spoke with remained. "They deserve to be taught to read and cipher to make their lives easier, while studying the Bible will lead them to God."

"They can attend church for that." Since he muttered the statement, Annette pretended she did not hear him.

"I will have Tubbs inspect the warehouse," she continued. "He is a decent carpenter. The opening date of the school will depend upon the amount of repairs required. I will need access to more of my funds, so I suggest you be prepared for those expenses."

A disagreeable look crossed his face, but the man nodded. "What income do you expect from this school?"

"None," she replied. "This will be free to the students."

He gasped. "Free! You will not get a return on your investment that way!"

"I am not looking for a monetary return."

"Sir Nigel would never approve such an expense!"

"I know." Annette remembered the times she had attempted to interest the old baronet in her school, only to be met with outright derision and refusal. "His opinion does not matter. The money is mine. All those papers I just signed prove it."

"I never heard of a school like that. At least, not around here."

Before such a weak argument, Annette rolled her eyes. "This is an age of innovation. I want to try something new."

She challenged him with a stare. Dropping his gaze to his desk, Keller picked up a quill. He ran the feather through his fingers and then sighed.

"Perhaps," he said. "But people do not change their ways easily. Your school may not be as accepted as you think. There could be resistance. May I offer you some advice?"

She looked at him. Both of them knew that country people were even slower to change their ways than the educated, and her students would come from that class. "What do you have in mind?"

"Set up a board of trustees to oversee your school."

"Trustees!" Annette was aghast. This was her idea. Her

dream. "I do not need or want anyone telling me how to run my school."

"If it is only you in charge, you may have trouble."

"The people around here know me."

"No matter how highly your reputation for good works is regarded around here, you are still a woman. Trustees can give you the protective authority. The people are familiar with an oversight board because of the poorhouses and the church."

"I do not want any interference."

He shrugged. "Most of these board positions are strictly ceremonial."

As she studied him, her eyes narrowed. "Whom did you have in mind for these sinecure positions?"

Keller tapped the quill against the desktop before replying. "I would recommend the vicar, the new baronet, and myself."

"The baronet?" She nearly squeaked out the name. "How could you choose him? You just told me how terrible his reputation is."

"No matter. His title naturally causes one to consider him. People in this area are used to looking up to the baronet. Even with a new baronet, his tacit approval as a trustee will smooth your work."

Annette wanted to argue with the solicitor, but she knew he was right. The three trustees he listed were the traditional leaders of the village. Country people were strong on tradition. They would distrust her new school less if those to whom they looked for leadership extended their approval.

She said, "I understand about the baronet. Since you named yourself, does this mean you changed your mind about my school?"

He inclined his head. "I would be willing to serve in the oversight position. Of course, I can assist you in managing its expenses, so that you get value for your money."

"I can handle the administration of the school on my own," she told him sharply. "Since I must bow to country custom, there will be a board of trustees, but I expect no interference from it."

"I understand." He rubbed his hands briskly. "Once you have asked the others, I will draw up the necessary papers."

She sighed at how complex her dream was becoming. "I will ask the vicar to join you."

"And the baronet?"

"Yes, him, too." To herself, she muttered, "Maybe he will say no."

But that hope had little life. She thought it all too likely Sir Gerard would relish the opportunity to interfere with her plans.

Sir Gerard pulled on the reins to halt Silver Shadow as the walls of Hathaway Hall came into view through the dark branches of the trees lining the road. The horse tossed his head in mild protest. Plainly he wanted his stall.

Sir Gerard also wanted to be warm and inside, but for the moment he was content to gaze upon his home. For so long he had waited to be the master of Hathaway Hall, that he needed to drink in the sight of it to confirm his ownership. Built at the end of the seventeenth century, the house stood atop a slight rise and was surrounded by a small park. Two wings jutted from the central section, protecting a stone-paved courtyard from the worst of the wind. At the top of the steps, the big wooden door barred the world outside. Although it was only noon, the day was overcast and there was a scent of a storm in the air. Candlelight winked from some of the windows, promising a warm reception within. The implied welcome cheered his heart.

From his spot on the drive, the place appeared to be under siege. His uncle had not cared for the expense involved to maintain a large amount of formal landscape. The dried remains of weeds cluttered the lawn. On this gray January day, it almost seemed as if the forest advanced upon the hall. The barren branches reached out to grasp the stone walls. Care had not been lavished upon the property during the previous baronet's tenure, even though repairs had been competently done. No one cheated his uncle out of his money. Sir Nigel may be only recently deceased, but life had long ago died behind the dull gray walls of Hathaway Hall.

Leaning forward to pat Silver Shadow's neck, Sir Gerard reflected on his plans for his home. At last, it was his home. Above all, he intended to make it the place he had always believed it could be.

After his father's death, he had been sent to live with his uncle. He had never admitted it to anyone, but originally he had looked forward to living with old Sir Nigel. Although only eleven years old, Gerard had already learned the impossibility of living up to his father's standards of perfect conduct, education, and piety. He had never won his father's approval, but he hoped his uncle would be different.

As a boy, Gerard had not realized the significance of the fact that his father and uncle were brothers and raised in the same strict tradition. He had only exchanged his place of residence. No love, no warmth existed at Hathaway Hall, only the same impossible standards that he continued to fail to meet. Even snatching a biscuit from the kitchen was punished as if it were practically a hanging offense. Meals of bread and water, accompanied by beatings with a switch, were bestowed upon him, but never approval.

The only refuge he found was in the stables. Nat the groom was gruff but not cruel. He did not have much use for people, yet the horses under his care had sleek coats and well-filled mangers. Gerard was in the stalls so often, Nat probably began to regard the boy as one of his animals. The groom taught him how to care for those under his care, and Gerard learned the lesson well. His skill with horses had earned him Silver Shadow. Despite his rank, he had been one of the cold and hungry. He resolved never to forget the horses or the people who were his responsibility.

When he reached his majority, he escaped to London, determined to toss aside his uncle's strictures and live according to his own rules, which involved wine, women, and wagering. His charm and willing attitude carried him far into social circles, but the lack of money curtailed his rebellion. He became a staple of society, a hanger-on who could be depended upon and therefore overlooked. He still waited for their admiration.

At last Hathaway Hall was his. For over a century it had stood. It belonged in the Wiltshire countryside, and it was respected by its neighbors. As the newest baronet, the respect should belong to him. Under his care, he would make the place thrive. He owed that to Nat's memory. He would prove wrong the judgments his father and uncle had made about him. Life could be enjoyed in frivolous pastimes without disaster befalling his heritage. Once he got his money back, he could set about restoring the hall and claim his rightful place in society.

With a clucking sound and a flick of the reins, Gerard nudged his horse forward again. When he arrived at the courtyard, he turned Silver Shadow over to the groom and climbed the few steps to the door, which Newton, the butler, promptly opened.

"Welcome back, sir." The tall, impassive man took his coat, folding it carefully before setting it down. The servant would brush the dirt away later.

Newton was too dignified to ask about the meeting with the solicitor, and Sir Gerard had no desire to tell of his defeat in breaking the will. Instead, he politely asked, "Did anything happen while I was gone?"

"You have a caller, sir."

"Who is it? Someone local, I presume." He tugged on his jacket.

"The man is not someone I recognize. He insisted on waiting for you, so I put him in the parlor."

From the butler's cold tone, Sir Gerard inferred the man was not a gentleman. "Who is he?"

The servant extended the silver tray with a calling card laying on it. The name read Mortimer Wallace. A sick feeling spread throughout Sir Gerard's stomach. The man was the money-lender to whom he owed thousands of pounds. The butler had correctly pegged him as no gentleman. Mr. Wallace regarded himself as a businessman. The fact that he now sat in Hathaway Hall's parlor did not bode well.

"Shall I tell him you are not at home?" the butler asked.

"No, if he has come all the way from London, he will stay until he speaks with me. Putting him off will do no good."

Squaring his shoulders, Sir Gerard took a deep breath and walked into the parlor. Mortimer Wallace did not immediately look up from the newspaper he was reading.

At such cavalier treatment, and in his own home, a surge of annoyance shot through Sir Gerard. "I am surprised to see you here," he said loudly.

Wallace slowly lowered the paper, and his well-filled face appeared over it. "Not the most welcoming greeting I have ever had," he observed as he carefully folded the *Times*. "But I will say how do you do, sir."

The man stood, and the chair creaked as his bulk was lifted. The tailored lines of his dark blue coat sought to reduce his waistline with extra padding in the shoulders, but the effect only increased his size. A double chin rested on a very white and very starched cravat. Elegance was not Mortimer Wallace's style, prosperity was. He extended a plump hand to the baronet.

Not wishing to offend the man, Sir Gerard shook it. The hand was as dry as the pound notes the money-lender piled up in his strongbox. "I had not expected to find you here," he said.

Without waiting for the invitation to do so, Wallace sat down again. The chair groaned. "Surely you knew I would keep a close eye on my money."

Dread cracked through Sir Gerard's heart. "Have you come for payment?"

Wallace cast a keen glance at him. "Could you pay me, if I demanded it?"

Sir Gerard swallowed, but sat down on another chair with a bored attitude. He lied, "I would have to sell some things to raise the ready, but it could be done."

The other man beamed at him with vast good will. "I am so very pleased to hear that. Based upon the expecta-

tions of your inheritance, you became my largest client."
Sir Gerard bowed his head in acknowledgment, as the
money-lender continued, "When all your eggs are in one
basket, you watch that chicken. Naturally, I wanted to
meet with you after the will had been read. Repayment is
always a concern in my business. Can you imagine my
surprise when gossip at the inn informed me all the money
went to some spinster? You have only the entail left."

Sir Gerard supposed he should have expected the unusual will to become a topic for local gossip, but it an-
gered him anyway that his troubles were discussed so
freely. "Tavern stories are seldom accurate."

"True, but it did heighten my concern. Did you inherit
Sir Nigel's fortune?"

There was no avoiding the direct question. "No. Some
local adventuress inherited from my uncle."

"Everything?"

"Not the entail, of course!" He examined his finger-
nails. It was becoming more difficult to maintain a bored
air.

The money-lender rubbed his hand along his chin in
thought. "This news concerns me greatly."

"I will repay you," Sir Gerard told him, even as he
wondered how.

Wallace beamed at him, but the baronet noticed no
humor in the man's gray eyes. "I am pleased to hear you
can meet your obligation to me."

Sweat began to break out under Sir Gerard's shirt, but
he managed to maintain a relaxed air. "The first payment
is not due until the end of this month."

"Just like a lord." The money-lender shook his head in
mock dismay. "You don't read the papers you sign." The
mask of geniality dropped from his fleshy face, and he

leaned forward. "Your note promises to repay the full amount whenever I demand it. I advanced you such a large sum because your uncle was known to be a wealthy miser, and he had just passed away, but I am not foolish with my money. Your prospects appear very poor to me now, and I am withdrawing the loan."

"You cannot do that! We had an agreement."

"True, and you agreed to repay me whenever I demanded it. I want my money back."

Sir Gerard rubbed his hands together to stop the numbness spreading through his body. How could he have signed such a loan? Ruin stared him in the face. "I cannot pay you now," he exclaimed. "Do you think I keep that kind of a sum in my strongbox? It will take time to gather the money together."

Wallace shrugged. "I can be a reasonable man. The first payment is due at the end of the month. I will accept the full amount then, instead."

"That's outrageous!"

The money-lender shrugged again. "That's business. I will forgo the extra interest I could have earned, in my concern to regain my principal. It is nothing personal against you."

In sick silence, Sir Gerard watched Wallace struggle to his feet. Where was he going to find the money to repay his debt? The loan he had so blithely signed now threatened to destroy him. The memories of the celebratory card games and racing bets filled him with bitterness.

The money-lender continued, "I had hoped to share a congenial brandy with you as you laid that rumor to rest. Instead, you only confirmed its accuracy, so I shall forgo the drink. I expect you to bring me your money at the end of the month. I *will* see you in London, sir."

Instinctively trained in good manners, Sir Gerard stood and responded to the man's farewell bow. When the parlor door had closed on Wallace's bulk and he was alone, the pose of unconcern fell away. His shoulders slumped as his brain scrambled to find a solution to his problem. His friend Linton needed money and so had none to lend. The solicitor had killed any hope of overturning the will. Perhaps the estate's rents could possibly meet the first payment, but he would be left with nothing to live on until the next quarter. Besides, even the rents could not repay his loan. It would take years, with a close eye kept on every expense. He did not have years.

With a groan, he went over to the fireplace and put his head on the mantelpiece. The flames flickering there could not warm the coldness freezing him inside. He had relied too heavily on his uncle's business interests to provide the income to restore Hathaway Hall. With the albatross he had hung around the estate, he could never care for his people. Despite all his hopes for respect and all his waiting, his dreams were finished before they even began.

A knock on the door stirred his attention. "Come in," he said listlessly.

The butler entered. "Miss Courtney has called, sir. Are you at home to her?"

Chapter Four

After leaving the solicitor's office, Annette refused to waste any time to discovering whether the baronet was going to be a trustee on her school board or not. She relied on the principle of doing an unpleasant task immediately.

Accordingly, she at once set off for Hathaway Hall along a path she had trod many times from Upper Brampton village. The trip did not take long. She eyed the darkening clouds in the distance. They threatened a storm, but she could conclude her business with Sir Gerard in a rapid fashion. After all, how long would it take him to refuse to be her school's trustee? It was not until the butler showed her into the parlor that the beginnings of trepidation gripped her.

"Good afternoon, Miss Courtney." The baronet greeted her with a polite smile on his face as he turned from his position by the fire. "It was good of you to call so quickly."

She stared at him in momentary confusion. Then she remembered his suggestion of a proposal, and embarrassment swept through her. Suddenly she was aware of how disorganized she must appear. The long tramp through the winter air had left her nose and cheeks red, while her hair tumbled down in a disorderly manner. She was in no condition to call on Sir Gerard, especially if he had a proposal to discuss.

Putting up a hand to tuck some of the wisps of her hair under her bonnet, she attempted a smile in return, but within she knew her bold determination had received a check. "It seems we have much to discuss. I saw no reason to wait."

He nodded. "Please sit here by the fire, while I request tea be made."

"Thank you. Tea would be very welcome." She took the wing chair closest to the blaze and remembered the solicitor had warned against listening to the baronet. He had labeled Sir Gerard *a charmingly persuasive man.* She prepared to hear the baronet's proposal, but she would not lose sight of her goal to build the school.

He settled himself into another chair also close to her and the fire. Crossing his legs at the ankles, he leaned back as if to examine her. She wanted to reach up to further adjust her hair, but resisted the urge. The prospect of a proposal was not going to turn her into a silly schoolgirl.

"Miss Courtney, although we have not known each other previously, my uncle's will has required us to become acquainted."

"That is true," she acknowledged. "I only know of you through your reputation."

His smile tightened, but he continued in a pleasant tone. "I, on the other hand, knew nothing of you until the reading of the will."

"Your uncle was not likely to mention me. Every time

I saw him, I asked for donations to care for the poor in our area."

"And now you have all the money you could ever want." There was a tinge of bitterness in his voice.

"I am very grateful."

"Yet, I do not have the money I expected."

Guilt at her good fortune inched through her body. "I did not ask for this bequest. It was as much a shock to me as to you."

"But you were the one who benefited," he pointed out. "It would only be fair if I received what was due me."

She eyed him warily. "What did you have in mind?"

No longer leaning back in his chair, he faced her. "I propose we make a settlement between us. You keep a sum of the money for your needs and wants, while I regain control of the rest. It is only justice to do so."

Laughter nearly bubbled from her lips, but she restrained it. How foolish her vanity was to even think he would be proposing marriage! She would always wear the label of spinster. Of course, a man with his wastrel reputation would not be one she would even consider marrying. Setting aside her foolish ideas to deal with practicalities, she asked him, "Why should I give you some of the money when I now have all of it?"

"It is a huge fortune. Much more than a woman like you could even consider handling."

He spoke with the patience she expected to use on her students, and it irritated her. "I would have you know, sir, that I am thirty years of age and long past the era of a giddy girlhood. I am quite capable of handling my affairs."

"Of course you are, but not at this magnitude." He stood and began to pace around the parlor. His strides wove a path around the chairs and tables arranged for warmth and conversation. "I have waited all my life to manage this estate, and I need the money to do it."

"Would you truly use it for the estate?" she asked. "Your reputation leads one to think otherwise."

He threw up his hands in dismay. "Always you mention my reputation. For a Christian woman, you believe an amazing amount of gossip."

She felt her face flush at this accusation. It was true that all she did know about Sir Gerard came from the rantings of his uncle. Sir Nigel may have been a wizard at making money, but he disliked people. He had even called *her* a money-grubber, which was not a strictly accurate name. She may have grubbed money from him, but it never benefited herself.

"I am sorry," she said. "I have been judging you based upon hearsay and am glad you want to help the people on the estate. They lead difficult lives. How did you intend to spend the money? I do know about the conditions here, if you would like my advice."

He smiled at her, and she noticed how distinguished he looked. His brown hair was carelessly dressed, but not slovenly. His face was lean with prominent high cheekbones. No fat bunched anywhere on his tall body, leading her to believe it had been gossip she listened to. A life of dissipation would have left some signs on a man of thirty-five years.

"You are a good woman," he said with a sincerity she easily heard in his voice. She had received that compliment many times before, most often from the rector or one of the people she helped, but never before had the words caused such a warm glow to surround her heart.

She smiled back. "Thank you."

A knock on the door signaled the arrival of the tea. She offered to pour, while he again sat in his chair. The tea aroma was pleasantly strong, promising a delicious cup. Apparently under the new master, no longer would reused tea leaves be offered to callers.

When the cups had been filled and the cakes tried, he said, "We will need to meet with the solicitor to transfer the money. I appreciate your generosity, and want the amount of the bequest remaining to you to be ample. Would five hundred pounds be sufficient?"

She nearly choked on her tea. "Five hundred! I need much more than that!"

"More!" He looked in amazement at her. "What on earth for? After you buy some dresses and pay off your bills, the amount left should be ample for your needs for the rest of your life."

Annette thought he had made a noble effort not to glance at her serviceable, but unfashionable dress, when he spoke that statement. Again, she wished she could have worn a pretty dress. Nevertheless, he must be told of her plans. "I want to open a school and called to ask if you would be on the board of trustees."

It was his turn to sputter in astonishment. "A school? For whom? Why?"

She set down her teacup. This topic was becoming familiar territory, and she could handle it with confidence. "The school will be for the local children so that they can be taught reading, writing, and ciphering."

His shocked brown eyes stared at her. "Why would you use my money to teach a pack of illiterate brats?"

Anger stirred within her at his ignorance. Her speech became even more precise as she replied, "They are only illiterate because they have never been taught to read. Education will change that. It will help them out of poverty."

"It will only give them ideas above their station," he fired back. He jumped to his feet and glared down at her. "The same way women get nonsensical notions when they are placed in charge of money."

She stood also, meeting his gaze directly at eye level. "I can handle a household, and I can certainly handle the money to run a school. You can watch me do it."

"You intend to spend the whole fortune on this school? It's outrageous! Will you be feeding them a roast at every meal?"

She felt herself flush at his disparagement. "I know how to make a farthing do the work of a penny. You need not fear that the school will not be run in a thrifty manner."

He scowled at her a moment longer, but her eyes did not waver. His glance fell away as he mastered his temper.

"Forgive me," he said. "You are obviously a woman quite capable of managing her own affairs. After all, my uncle dealt with you many times and was familiar with your tenacious tendencies. Perhaps it was to keep his afterlife quiet that he left you the money."

The attempt at humor was forced, but Annette recognized it as an effort to reestablish polite footings, and she smiled. "Perhaps I did badger him more than he liked."

"Does anyone like to be badgered?" he asked. Amusement lurked in his eyes, inviting her response.

"No, I think not. Even I do not care for it."

They gazed at each other with rueful acknowledgment of the truth. Annette was determined not to be too quick to judge Sir Gerard this time. Naturally he would be upset at losing the fortune he expected, but his anger had flared only briefly before his good humor reasserted itself.

Attempting to maintain their cordiality, she said, "I will use the money wisely. The school will not be wasteful, and the results will please you."

He ran a hand through his hair, but its disarrangement still looked fashionable. "You asked me to be a trustee, did you not?"

Alarm cautioned her. Had she mistaken his amicable air for further trouble? "Yes. Mr. Keller explained it would be customary to have a board overseeing the school. He suggested yourself and the Reverend Brown as members. He has already agreed to be one."

"I will take you up on your offer," he told her. "As a trustee, I can verify that you are doing as you promised with your school."

"I keep my word." Annette tugged at her gloves. "Now that my purpose here is finished, I must be going. Thank you for the tea and for agreeing to be one of my trustees."

"I intend to be a very watchful one," he assured her. "But I believe that if anyone can teach those brats, it will be you."

Once again, she exchanged smiles with him. Although she had dreaded this meeting with him, Sir Gerard was much easier to deal with than his uncle. His manner was more pleasant, and when necessary, he possessed the grace to admit he was wrong. She thought she would not fear any future encounters with the baronet quite so much. They might even be pleasant.

For the first time, she looked out the drawing room window. The outside had darkened and lazy snowflakes drifted down. Either she had stayed longer than intended, or that storm cloud had arrived faster than expected. Her walk home would certainly be wet and cold. It might even be dangerous. Annette bit her lip. The wisest course would be to ask for a carriage to take her. After all her proclamations about being capable enough to handle the fortune, the prospect galled her. Still, she would speak as she must.

"I find I must request another favor, sir," she said. "May I borrow a carriage to return me home?"

A frown furrowed Sir Gerard's brow. "You did not walk here, did you?" he demanded.

"Yes, I did. It is the way I am used to traveling," she explained. Some of her habits would have to change.

"You can now afford to keep a coach and horses," he reminded her.

"Yes, sir." She agreed and felt laughter beginning to dance within her. "I will tend to that directly, as soon as I am home."

"I will order my carriage out to take you," he said.

"Thank you." Her grateful demureness did not fool him.

He waved a finger at her in admonishment. "You are a managing woman, Miss Courtney."

"So I have been told." She tried to remain humble, but she again saw the merriment in his eyes. What was it about this man that made her want to laugh?

He shook his head. "To make certain you arrive home safely, I will escort you in the coach."

Her eyes widened. "Without a chaperone?"

"Do not turn missish on me now, Miss Courtney. A woman with your strength of character has her virtue as a chaperone."

She looked at him a little uncertainly. She had intended to request a ride home from him, but it had been no part of her plans that he would come along. In too many ways, he acted contrary to what she expected. She was a managing woman and proud of her ability, yet Sir Gerard unsettled her, and that disturbed her.

The baronet opened the drawing room door for her as they stepped into the front hall. Despite everything else, Annette could not fault him for his manners. He made her feel like someone important. Even as she assured herself he was only being polite, she could not deny the tiny thrill of delight that sparked through her at his attention.

When the butler appeared with her cloak, Sir Gerard was the one who assisted her. The baronet's movements were sure as he settled the wool over her shoulders, enclosing her within the folds of cloth that no longer seemed familiar. Abruptly, she stepped away from him and finished fastening the cloak.

The butler helped Sir Gerard shrug into his coat and handed his gloves and hat to him. Even with the extra thickness of wool necessary for warmth, the frame of his body retained its essence of elegance. He held out his arm to escort, and she rested her hand upon it. He placed his own atop hers. She felt his strength through her gloves. His grasp was firm, but not tight.

When she went down the steps, she knew no fear of slipping on the stones. He would keep her safe. It was a novel idea to Annette. She was used to caring for herself and others. He assisted her into the carriage and then climbed in beside her.

She stiffened, realizing how much of the seat he took and how small the carriage was. The storm clouds had darkened what little natural light the winter afternoon would have provided. Although not pitch-black inside, Sir Gerard's face was obscured and his body a darker shade.

However, he was not indistinct like a shadow. She was very aware of his presence in the carriage.

With a jolt, they jerked forward and the trip began. To himself, Sir Gerard smiled with amusement. In the gloom, he could see Miss Courtney sitting stiff as a poker, her hands tightly clasped on her lap. He doubted she held them there for warmth. A typical spinster, thinking every man ready to attack her. She was safe in his company. He preferred his women to be far more sophisticated and witty. Yet, this one held his fortune, so he would woo her as if she were someone other than a managing old maid.

He began a conversation with his companion just as if they were seated at a fashionable dinner party. "Have you lived all your life in Upper Brampton?"

"Almost all of it. When I was very young, my father obtained this living. After he died, my mother and I continued here because it was familiar and my mother became ill."

"Your father was the rector?" he inquired politely. "When was that?"

"He died about twelve years ago." She sighed. "He was a very good man and taught me to care for my fellow man."

"A good lesson for a rector to teach," he commented. "Your father must have been here when I was sent to live with my uncle after my parents died."

"Did you ever meet him?" Excitement tinged her voice as if she were eager to share her father with him. "Was he the one who prepared you in your studies before you went off to school? Or did you have a private tutor?"

In spite of himself, Sir Gerard laughed. Her assumptions about his uncle's care were so wide of the mark. "No, Miss Courtney, there was no private tutor nor did I study with your father. Uncle Nigel did not want the cost involved, and a young boy can be expensive to teach."

"But he sent you to school?"

Sir Gerard heard the perplexity in her voice, even though the darkness prevented him from seeing it on her face. "The very fact that you are puzzled tells me you grew up in a loving family. My uncle did not want me around. He only took on my care because the law required it, and I was his heir. He never spent one farthing on me that was not extorted from him. You, above all, should know how tight he was with his money."

"That is true," she acknowledged, "but you still ended up educated."

He was not surprised she did not understand. How could she? The carriage continued jolting over the rough road to the village. A sudden dip caught him off balance. He banged his head against the wooden back. The sudden pain brought him back to his senses. What was he doing talking about the rejected lad he had been so many years ago? He was thirty-five now. There was no need to recall the past.

"Yes, Uncle Nigel did educate me." He grasped for the strap to maintain his balance and added with bitter humor, "I think he discovered the expense of a school outweighed the discomfort I caused him at home."

"He only spent his money on his comfort," she observed. "The tenants on the estate suffered much under his austerity. I did what I could getting donations, but their need is so immense."

"You must have impressed my uncle, or he would not have left you the money." He still considered her a managing spinster, but he now realized she was not an adventuress. She truly believed in helping the poor, although he doubted her idea of a school would work. The ignorance was too great.

"I hope you will care for your people better," she said.

Through the shadows, he could feel her gaze upon him. Again he was being assessed, judged whether or not he would measure up. This time, though, she asked about something he had long wanted to do. He had waited his whole life to become the baronet so he could be the one to set things right.

"I want to help them," he told her. The sincerely made declaration felt good because it was the truth. He had not forgotten the lessons Nat the groom taught him in the stables.

"There is much that needs doing. I am glad you are not like your uncle portrayed you. He was very wrong, and Upper Brampton is very fortunate you are the new baronet."

Pride swelled within him. Praise for his qualities was an unusual occurrence. It was not only his uncle who named him a wastrel; there were those in London who looked down on him for his avoidance of betting. He never participated in the outrageous dares that amused the men of his set. He had only gone to Mortimer Wallace for an advance to celebrate his first chance to fully participate in society's follies. The actual folly was how his lack of foresight caused him to gamble so wastefully before the money was in his possession. He thinned his lips. He did not want to ruin her positive image of him by mentioning the money-lender.

"I have been away in order to avoid my uncle," Sir Gerard told her. "I will need advice on how to help these people, and I believe you are the one capable of telling me."

She tossed back her head and laughed. "No one has ever accused me of not having an opinion. I will be happy to express my ideas to you."

"Express away," he told her as a whiff of violet perfume drifted to his nose.

The tension in the carriage seemed to have lessened. Although the passing of the sun made it darker, Sir Gerard discovered he felt more at ease with this spinster. The darkness had forced an intimacy of feeling between them, but he did not feel threatened by the empathy.

Her mood turned serious as she continued, "I have already told you about my plans for a school, but the tenants on your estate need more help than that. Their houses are in a state beyond dilapidation. I do not believe a single repair was done on them during your uncle's entire tenure. At least, not in the past several years. Roofs are leaking, and chimneys are in a dangerous state. The necessary repairs will be extensive."

He nodded before he realized she could not see that response. "It will be difficult to do everything."

"I think once you make a beginning, the tenants will understand it takes time to recover from decades of neglect."

"What I meant, is that to make the repairs will be so expensive." He looked over at the dark form, trying to gauge her mood. "My uncle's money is very necessary for these projects."

He felt her stiffen in rejection. "I will use the money responsibly," she said.

"But this is its purpose," he said. "Do you not want to help these people?"

"Of course." Her enunciation turned precise. "My school will not be wasteful."

In his anger and fear, he exploded. "Forget your school for a moment! I need the money. You must give it back to me."

She did not shrink from him. Even though he could not see her eyes, he knew her gaze stared directly at him without fear. "Your uncle left the money to me. I will use it for my school and elsewhere—to help the unfortunate. I will be responsible for it. You can spend your money on the estate. It brings in quite a bit in rent."

He nearly laughed. Or was it a sob? He did not know or care. She thought he had other resources. How could she know he faced ruin for his debts? The estate had no rents coming due any time soon. His uncle had died after the quarter payments were made, and those monies were part of the fortune this spinster inherited. Hathaway Hall's farms would not provide any income until the next quarter. He could not wait that long.

"Miss Courtney, please, can we not come to a settlement? By all rights, that money belongs to me. I am willing to be reasonable and leave an ample amount in your care. I will even fund your school," he added desperately.

"I appreciate your offer," she said, "but my school is already fully funded."

The carriage jerked to a halt. They had arrived at her home. The servant climbed down and opened the door. She gathered her skirts and stepped out. Before leaving, she turned to curtsy to him. "Thank you for the ride home. I am grateful I did not have to walk and shall check into acquiring a carriage of my own."

Then the door slammed shut, and he was alone. The blackness in the carriage was nothing compared the blackness of the abyss of ruin before him. All his life he waited to be in this position of respect, yet because of a miserly old man and the stubbornness of one woman, his dreams would be destroyed.

The carriage rolled down the main street of the village. Distracted, he gazed out the window at the stores and homes.

When the vehicle passed the inn, he could see into the lighted upper room set aside for private dining. Inside he saw Mortimer Wallace seated before a rich repast. Despite the sight of so many deliciously cooked dishes, Sir Gerard felt a sick nausea settle in his stomach that had nothing to do with the jerking movements of the carriage. Until the end of the month. That was all the time remaining before the money-lender destroyed his dreams.

Chapter Five

Annette discovered she enjoyed being an heiress. It was pleasant to pay off her debts owed to the shop-keepers. No longer did she worry about ducking into the store to buy a necessity. Now, wide smiles and welcoming bows from the merchants greeted her.

When Annette donated enough to the church to replace the leaking roof, the vicar's praise for her generosity swelled to the old rafters. His effusiveness embarrassed her. She had long known the needs of the church and the rest of the district. At last she had the opportunity to do something about both of them.

The universal approval that met her actions soothed any doubt in her heart that Sir Gerard's demands might have created. She told herself, "I am using the money wisely."

Her greatest pleasure came the day she tramped over the musty cold warehouse with the carpenter. Wisps of straw blown about by the wind whistling through the bigger cracks in the walls covered the floor. A large puddle in one corner had frozen into an indoor skating rink. Even the mice, certainly inhabiting the walls, stayed hidden for warmth. Rubbing her hands together to stay warm, Annette knew she would have to add a chimney and stove to her plans.

The carpenter Tubbs assessed the damage and his client before quoting a price to repair the roof and the walls.

Annette's gasp of surprise echoed in the hollow building. "That's an outrageous price!"

The burly man shrugged. "Lot of work to be done."

"I am aware of that, but your price is too high."

"I need help with some of this bigger work. I have to pay them, too," the carpenter pointed out.

Annette gazed directly at him, her hands on her hips. "Now, Tubbs, I know times are hard and prices are high. I also know I have the money to pay you a decent wage, and that is what I am going to do. Pay you a decent wage, not allow highway robbery."

He scuffed his feet against the dirt coating the floor. "You been good to me and my family many times, Miss Courtney. I don't forget that."

The adjusted price he named was far more reasonable, and with a little bit more negotiation, they reached a rate acceptable to both of them.

Annette shook his hand. "I want to open the school as soon as possible, so do your best."

"For you, I will."

His promise reassured her. Tubbs was a man who kept his word. With pleased expectation, Annette gazed around the warehouse. A few empty barrels remained of the former inventory. Soon her benches filled with children would replace the dark emptiness. The sound of recitations would resound in the bare space as the students learned their arithmetic and reading. She sighed with happiness at the prospect. Her dream of a school finally seemed within reach.

The only area where Annette did not exert control was her social life. Here, to her dismay, her companion Lucille dominated.

"The first thing we must do," Lucille stated, "is to make your wardrobe more fashionable. More color would not be a bad idea, either."

They were visiting the dressmaker's place, and the woman had just placed a nice length of brown wool before them. Annette liked the cloth.

"This looks very serviceable," she told her companion. "The brown will not show the dirt, and the fabric appears strong enough to wear well."

Lucille sniffed in contempt. "Service is not something we are looking for." Her gaze assessed the bolts stacked at the back. She marched over to a dark green silk and ran her hand over it. "This looks very nice. You would like a gown sewn from it."

Mrs. Hutchens, the dressmaker, blinked in surprise behind her round glasses. A tall, spare woman with her brown and gray hair pulled back from her face, she dressed in the clothes she sewed, providing an excellent model for her creations. A pleased smile spread across her face as she sailed over to join Lucille. "Forgive me. I did not realize you wanted an evening gown."

Neither did Annette. She tried to interfere. "I have two perfectly good gowns already."

Lucille did not even turn around from her inspection of the bolts. "Pshaw! You have worn those to such threads that I am amazed they still hold together. You need something new to wear for the Assembly."

Mrs. Hutchens nodded in agreement. "If you wish, I can sew it in time for the next one."

Annette raised her eyebrows at this statement. "It always took almost a month to make one of my gowns before."

"But an evening gown is ever so much more important," the dressmaker said.

The price would probably reflect the extra work, Annette supposed. All other thoughts vanished when the woman unrolled a length of deep blue silk shot through with silver threads. Annette's breath caught in her throat at the sight of the shimmering fabric.

Unable to stop herself, she reached out to caress the smooth, cool cloth. It spilled through her hands as though the night sky unfolded before her. For an instant, she wondered how Sir Gerard would regard her in a gown created from this silk. Would he see someone more than the spinster everyone considered her to be?

"You like this one?" Mrs. Hutchens asked.

There was no need for Annette to pretend otherwise. Her hands still played with the fabric. "Yes. How much does it cost?"

"Two guineas a yard, plus the cost of the sewing."

Annette gasped. "Two guineas!"

The dressmaker defended herself. "It is a fair price. The silk was smuggled all the way from France. There is no duty included."

"Excellent!" Lucille declared. "We will buy enough to make a gown from that. It will be the first one we want made up, but we shall choose the design later."

"But . . ." Annette tried to protest she did not want to encourage smuggling, but Lucille had commanded Mrs.

Hutchens's attention. The women ignored her as they turned back to examine the fabrics.

"I do like this green silk," Lucille said. "It would also look good on Miss Courtney."

After choosing the evening dress fabrics, they selected others for day gowns. When Lucille and Mrs. Hutchens pored over the patterns, Annette offered an occasional opinion. It was usually disregarded. Lucille's wishes determined the designs for their clothes.

Despite, or perhaps because of, the large order they left with the dressmaker, Mrs. Hutchens was able to finish both the elegant blue and silver gown for Annette and the deep gold one Lucille had set her heart on for herself in a record time of three weeks.

Annette had spent the time overseeing the repairs to the warehouse, while Lucille supervised the sewing of their evening dresses. Acting with the same speed of the dressmaker, the carpenter Tubbs was able to renovate the building without delay. He employed a large crew of men eager for work. Sooner than she expected, her school was ready to open.

No thoughts of her dream intruded on her mind when Annette stood outside the Assembly room ready to make her entrance; rather a fluttering of nervousness capered within her. This was the first time she was appearing at a social gathering since her inheritance, and she felt like a young girl just beginning her debut. These people were her lifelong neighbors, but would they regard her differently now? She had already seen ample signs of how the money was changing her life. The very gown she wore offered proof.

Then her name and Lucille's were announced. Annette did not imagine the brief pause in the conversation as she felt every eye turn towards her. She lifted her chin and tried to pretend she did not notice. The music continued to play. After that short hesitation, the guests returned to their flirtations and gossip. Annette unfurled her fan with seeming unconcern, but her hand trembled. She had done nothing wrong. Yet, for a moment, she had felt pilloried beneath the assessing gazes of her neighbors.

The feeling did not last. It did not take long for the various men in the gathering to appear beside her, requesting a dance. Some of the bolder ones asked for two. With a lightness foreign to her, Annette laughed off those beseeching for more than one. She knew why she had suddenly become the belle of the ball.

From young Daniel Talbot, who had barely escaped from school, to widower Mr. Deschamps with four children, the motives of the single men were no puzzle at all. However, it shocked her when several of the married men also requested dances. After a moment she realized her money attracted them, too. Not for marriage, but for the investments she could fund.

Annette laughed and enjoyed her popularity to the fullest, with her eyes wide open. The only thing to mar her enjoyment was that her popularity did not extend to Lucille.

Her companion sat off to the side, a bewildered look on her face. With her congenial nature, Lucille was not often ignored at social gatherings. She had even been more excited about her new dress than Annette had been. Now Annette ached for her friend's hurt. She tried to have some attention turned to Lucille. All her hints about how the other woman enjoyed dancing, too, met with studied ignorance by her partners.

Then Sir Gerard Montfort joined the court clustered

around her. He dressed in a formal black coat sewn with the elegance only a London tailor could master, yet an air of ease emanated from him. The gold of his watch chain gleamed in the candlelight, emphasizing the black ebony of his coat. A smile lit his face.

Her heart seemed to pause before beating again at a much faster pace. Suddenly Annette knew her fears at the beginning of the Assembly had nothing to do with her reception by her neighbors and had everything to do with how this man would regard her in her new dress.

She managed a tolerably cool greeting. "Good evening, sir."

He bowed. "Good evening, Miss Courtney. I hope you saved a dance for me."

"I have promised so many," she replied with honest regret.

"All?"

When she looked up into his brown eyes, she knew more than anything, she wanted to dance one set with this London society man. "There is still the supper dance."

"Excellent! I not only have the chance to dance with you, I may take you to supper."

A thrill sparkled through her at the prospect. The fact that he greeted it with pleasure only deepened her anticipation.

The musicians struck a warning chord, announcing the start of the next dance. Annette's partner, the widower Mr. Deschamps, approached, and Sir Gerard started to turn away.

Afterwards, Annette did not know how she came to be so daring as to stop the baronet with the request, "Please, wait."

Sir Gerard halted. "Yes?"

Annette swallowed and then spoke in a rush, almost slurring her words together. "My companion, Mrs. Lucille Downes, she does not have a partner for this dance."

At his surprised look, heated mortification flushed her cheeks and spread through her. Then she remembered how eagerly Lucille had looked forward to this night. Her friend had never anticipated being a wallflower, and now her expected pleasure had been disappointed. Previous hints to other partners had not worked, so Annette had made her request plain.

"You want me to dance with her?"

Annette heard surprise in his voice, though not an instant refusal. "Lucille is not usually a wallflower. She can be so charming and witty that usually partners cluster around her."

Sir Gerard held up his hand as if to halt the flow of words. "You have already convinced me, Miss Courtney. I will do as you ask."

There was no more time to speak. Her partner stood by, an eager expression on his face, and his arm extended to lead her onto the floor. As she went, Annette noticed Sir Gerard bowing before Lucille, and then her friend's face lightening with pleasure.

The dance was a vigorous reel. As she swung around, Annette was able to catch glimpses of the other couple. Once she heard Lucille's giggle above the music. Laughter was as much her friend's partner as the baronet.

Annette noticed Sir Gerard, too, seemed to take pleasure in the dance. He smiled and paid attention to his partner's remarks. One of his sallies earned him a light tap of reproof from Lucille's fan. His answering smile showed it did not appear to bother him. Even from across the dance floor, Annette could tell that Lucille did not mean it.

A warm glow spread within Annette that had nothing to do with the vigorousness of the dance. For her friend's sake, she was glad she had been so bold.

When the dance ended with a flourish of music, Annette realized she had paid more attention to Sir Gerard and Lucille than to her own partner. To make amends, the smile she bestowed on Mr. Deschamps was warmer than she intended. He responded with a squeeze of her hand. She remembered he had one wife in the graveyard and four lively children. As much as she wanted a family, his was not the one she desired.

The eager approach of her next partner saved her. Since he was a married man, he wanted to talk about money to improve his lands. The topic interested Annette because she knew how cruelly the cold winter and rise in prices were hurting the people of the area. Still, she could not linger with him. The next dance set and partner awaited.

And so it went throughout the evening. A brief partnering and then a switch. She almost became dizzy with the pace of it. She noticed that after the initial dance with the baronet, Lucille snagged several more partners and her friend's face now wore its typical happy expression.

Annette also managed to keep track of Sir Gerard. After dancing with Lucille, he partnered several other ladies, both married and single. However, he never danced more than once with any of them. Nor did he head for the card room and the betting games going on within there.

As her feet flew in the steps of the cotillions and polkas, she puzzled over the baronet's behavior. The story of his wastrel reputation was well entrenched, but he did not act in any such manner.

She had not satisfactorily resolved the problem by the time the supper dance arrived. Like all her previous partners, Sir Gerard appeared promptly at her side to claim his turn with her. "I believe this is our dance, Miss Courtney."

The breathlessness Annette felt had nothing to do with the amount of unaccustomed dancing she had done. Still, she managed to respond, "Indeed it is, sir."

Maybe it was the London tailoring that made him appear so elegant. Maybe it was the way the candlelight shadowed and illuminated the planes of his face. Maybe it was the smile that curved his lips that made her heart race faster. There was no time to study the phenomenon.

When Sir Gerard extended his arm to escort her to the floor, she lightly placed her hand upon it. She was proud to be his partner. After all, he was a London gentleman, and a very elegant one at that. He knew the steps and guided her confidently but vigorously without breathing heavily. Once again, the discrepancy between his card-playing reputation and what she observed disturbed her.

The dance moved too fast for her to gather her thoughts. The bits and pieces she knew about him whirled around with the same intensity as the reel she danced. Conversation was not possible as they switched partners in the set. Still, every time she glanced at him, he had a smile ready to bestow on her. The charm she had seen him use on his previous partners, he now lavished upon her twofold. Her feet flew beneath her skirts in the lively pattern of the reel, but her heart flew even faster.

When the musicians struck the final notes of the reel, Annette panted to get her breath back. Sir Gerard looked as alert and elegant as ever. His starched cravat appeared in no danger of wilting. It was a talent surely cultivated by attending years of London parties.

Annette plied her fan with more vigor than grace in an effort to cool herself. "Thank you for the dance."

"You are a most pleasant partner. I find I am enjoying this Assembly far more than I expected." He offered his arm to lead her to the supper table.

To avoid being distracted by the strength beneath her hand, she attempted to take him to task for his words. "You feared we were not as sophisticated as your London parties?"

"You are not." Before she could bristle at the implied affront, he continued, "I think that is part of the attraction. One can have fun without worrying about one's place."

"But surely, sir, you know we are all studying the new baronet in our midst so we can learn about London's ways and fashions."

He laughed, and she was surprised at how flirtatious she felt. "I am far from being an arbitrator of society," he told her.

"But here in Upper Brampton you are."

Curious, he glanced at her. "Are you trying to convince me to stay, Miss Courtney?"

The thought had not entered her mind, but now that he expressed it, she found she would be disappointed when he left. Not daring to speak such a thought, she plied her fan again. "Do you intend to stay?"

A tense look crossed his face that she had no chance to study. He drew her attention to the array of food spread before them. Oranges from the hothouse stacked like pyramids lay between the plates of sliced ham and sweetmeat balls. Tender rolls of bread were piled on the serving platters. Sliced pineapple surrounded flaky lobster tarts.

Impressed, Sir Gerard eyed the delicacies. "Miss Courtney, if this is a sample of how the people in Upper Brampton frolic, I will be very tempted to stay."

She laughed at his reply, yet she wondered at the momentary strained expression she had spotted when she had mentioned his returning to London.

Displaying another one of the talents he must have learned during his London rounds, Sir Gerard lead her to a small table where only the two of them could sit.

Once they were seated, Sir Gerard asked her, "Are you planning a trip to London soon?"

She shook her head. "No. My school will keep me busy."

"I would think a chance to shine in London would be a greater attraction than a village school."

"The school has been a dream of mine for years. London has not."

"I fear I must disbelieve that," he protested. "Every young girl must dream of making a shining debut in London."

Shrugging, Annette picked up a roll and buttered it. "Perhaps, if I had had a debut as a young girl, I would think differently." At the interest she saw on his face, she continued, "My father was the vicar here before the Reverend Brown. My mother was not very strong, so I discharged many of the duties regarding the poor in the parish."

"Including weaning money from my uncle."

She glanced cautiously at him, but the ghost of a smile curving his lips made her smile in response. "Most definitely including getting money from Sir Nigel. There is great need around here, especially with the rise in prices and the harsh winter." She shivered at the memory of the drafts in her own home. Disregarding the tempting food before her, she leaned towards him to convince him of her sincerity. "I know I have the fortune, and I can use it to educate the children. It will help them in the future, but you must take care of the estate's needs now."

He stiffened, and she recognized the wary look on his face. It reminded her of his uncle whenever she met him.

"Where do you think the money for the estate will come from?" he asked.

Puzzled, she blinked at him. "Why, from your own funds I would expect. And the estate will continue to produce an income."

"You already have this quarter's rents," he reminded her.

"Yes, but the end of March is only two months away."

His fork pushed a piece of ham around the rim of his plate. "If the need is so great, perhaps you should return my inheritance to me now, or even a portion of it, instead of forcing me to wait the two months."

Disappointed, she sank back against her chair. "I am not forcing *you* to wait for anything. It is the people under your care whom I am concerned about."

He stabbed at a piece of ham with his fork. "You have a big heart for everyone in need, don't you, Miss Courtney?"

"I try to," she replied.

"Perhaps I *need* the money more than they do." His brown eyes looked straight into hers. For an instant, she almost believed she saw desperation in their depths.

Then she gave herself a little shake, breaking the momentary bond between them. He certainly had the skill to charm her into believing what he wanted. Yet he acted like a miser, just like his uncle, unwilling to spend a shilling on those in desperate need. Obviously he had money. She had only to look at his elegant, and very stylish, coat, and the gold watch chain dangling from his waistcoat pocket. A signet ring adorned one finger. Back in his stables, she remembered, waited that magnificent gray stallion she had seen him riding. If she gave him the fortune, she doubted he would spend it as wisely as she would.

She laughed lightly. "If you were truly in need, perhaps I would help you."

The beginning bars of a dance melody sounded as the musicians reminded the company the supper was over. An immediate bustle filled the room as people pushed back their chairs.

"I will hold you to that." Sir Gerard stood and prepared to escort her back to the ballroom floor. Her time with him was over. Pasting a smile on her face, she joined him.

Soon the dance whirl caught her in its grip again. Somehow, even as she danced and laughed with her partners, she could not forget that glimpse of desperation she thought she had read in Sir Gerard's eyes.

Her gaze kept straying to the baronet. Sir Gerard was not a man who should appeal to her, yet she could not ignore him. Too frivolous claimed his reputation, but it occurred to her that all stories she had heard about him came from Sir Nigel. She spotted him looking at her and glanced away quickly. Soon though, she looked at him again.

She noticed the baronet had not disappeared into the card room throughout the entire evening. Certainly a man given to a life of dissipation could not so completely ignore the temptation. The contrast disturbed her because she was unable to pigeonhole him. Therefore, neither could she forget him.

For his part, Sir Gerard kept eyeing the spinster. Although he partnered other matrons and young girls, it was the annoying Miss Courtney who held his attention. She was so eager to do good according to her ideas that she overlooked *his* need.

When he made a trip to the punch bowl to fortify himself to continue with his social duty, he met his friend Linton.

"There you are!" he hailed Sir Gerard with a toast of his glass. "You must try this punch. These locals know how to make it."

The glazing of the other man's eyes hinted at the punch's potency, but its strength still surprised Sir Gerard. This arrack recipe plainly called for more than the usual amount of brandy along with its spices. The vintage was a good one, probably smuggled from France. He had discovered another reason for the popularity of the Upper Brampton Assemblies.

Sir Gerard felt the punch warm him as it slid down his throat. "This is good," he agreed. "Are you doing much dancing?"

"Some," Linton admitted. "I am trying to spot the dowered lasses."

"Don't be too obvious about it, or you will be labeled a fortune hunter."

Linton shrugged. "That's what I am—and you are, too."

A spurt of anger flashed through Sir Gerard. "Not by choice!"

His friend shrugged again. "Does anyone ever choose such a position?" He sipped from his glass. "Now that she has inherited, that Miss Courtney is the best plum available. This is probably the first time she has ever been the belle of the ball—and at her age, too."

Sir Gerard frowned. She had worn the violet perfume again, and he was discovering it a clue to the sweetness of her nature. The meanness in Linton's words besmirched the memory. "Let her enjoy herself. It is a small enough pleasure to begrudge her."

Linton's eyes had trouble focusing on his friend. "I say. You have certainly changed your tune. Don't you remember she cheated you from your uncle's money? I'm the one on your side."

"Cheated seems too strong a word. I think she was as surprised by the bequest as I was." He remembered the compassion for others he had heard in her life story. Knowing what had been left unsaid, he realized she had sacrificed her girlhood to care for her mother. In a lower tone, he added, "Unless you mean that perhaps life has cheated her."

"What's that you say? I didn't hear you."

Sir Gerard did not answer Linton. Instead, he grabbed the man by the arm and pulled him towards the dance floor. "Come. We need to find some partners for this next set."

Chapter Six

The punch had been potent, but Sir Gerard discovered a brisk ride the next morning on Silver Shadow chased away the wisps of its effects. After a quick canter across a fallow meadow, he reined in his horse and filled his lungs with the sharp tang of a winter morning in the woods. The rising sunlight shone through the barren branches of the surrounding trees, causing the air to warm and cool as he passed in and out of the shade. The smell of the rich earth stirred up by his stallion's hooves promised winter was only temporary.

Like his current problems. He patted Silver Shadow's neck. "What do you think, boy?" he asked the horse. "After all these years of living by my wits, am I going to be reduced to being a fortune hunter to regain my own wealth? Linton said it was the only way, but I cannot believe him. Marriage is not the solution. There must be another way."

The horse nickered as if he understood but offered no solution.

Sir Gerard stayed a moment longer, surveying the meadow with its tall brown grasses swaying in the slight breeze. This clearing, at least, was his. Part of the nearly two hundred entailed acres his uncle could not snatch from him. A pride of ownership swelled within him. This was his.

With renewed confidence, he nudged the stallion to head home. What he was going to do, he did not know, but an opportunity would arise. It always did.

After seeing to Silver Shadow's care in the stable, Sir Gerard strode into the house. The dimness of the hall caused him to blink after the bright sunlight, but the brisk coolness of the morning seemed to cling to him even after the butler took his overcoat and gloves.

Still enjoying the invigoration of his daybreak exercise, Sir Gerard asked, "Is Mr. Linton awake yet?"

"I believe he is in the library, sir."

The baronet started in that direction, when Newton's harrumph signaled he had more to say.

Sir Gerard paused. "Yes?"

"Sir, I wanted to remind you about the trustees' visit to the new village school for this afternoon."

He had forgotten all about it in the three weeks since Miss Courtney's visit. "Yes, of course. I will be there." He would have to be, if he intended to keep an eye on the school's expenditures. One could only hope that spinster knew enough to keep the costs under control.

His good mood banished, Sir Gerard stalked into the library. It was a little room, with a sense of closeness caused by the shelves crammed with books. Small tables stood near several chairs scattered about on the green rug. They were meant to hold the light for reading, but Sir Gerard spotted a brandy decanter on the table next to the chair in which Linton slumped.

His friend had obviously changed from the formal

clothes of the evening before, but a night's rest had not restored his outlook. He cast a bleary glance at the baronet and raised his glass in acknowledgment. The scent of the brandy wafted to Sir Gerard's nose, and he wrinkled it. Striding over to the table, he picked up the decanter. "Didn't you have enough of this stuff last night?"

"Apparently not," Linton mumbled. "My future looks just as bleak this morning."

Looking at the man, Sir Gerard could well believe that if not bleak, his friend's outlook was certainly blurry. Linton's drinking disappointed him. He set the decanter on a table out of Linton's reach. "I am sorry I cannot help you with your financial difficulties. I truly meant to."

His friend waved the apology away, causing the brandy to slosh in his glass. "You're my best friend. I won't forget you wanted to help." He toasted the baronet again and then gave a bitter laugh. "But you're in the same boat I am. You're a fortune hunter, too."

"I don't like that name," Sir Gerard answered sharply.

Linton shrugged. "It's the truth. Need to be leg shackled. Only marriage can save us now."

Sir Gerard turned away, not liking to hear his own morning thoughts so crudely spoken. "There must be another way."

"What?" His friend paused, but there was no reply. "At least, you have an heiress in sight. I have no one."

Sir Gerard did not pretend to misunderstand. He strode over to the fireplace mantel and stared down at the fire burning there. "I do not want to marry Miss Courtney."

"What choice do you have?"

At this moment Sir Gerard could see none, but that did not mean one did not exist. He had lived by his wits for too long not to find a solution to this problem.

How could he marry the spinster? She might not be the conniving adventuress he had first thought, but she still was not suitable as a wife. He amended the thought, *At least not for me.*

He knew what he required in a wife: both money and town polish. As a society hostess, the future Lady Westcourt needed connections and a strong will. He was willing to concede Miss Courtney had the will, but not the connections. Where was the necessary polish to overlook aristocratic transgressions? Gloomily he knew she was a woman of impeccable moral integrity.

His hand clenched the mantel, and he eyed the tempting decanter. He shook his head. Forgetfulness in drink would not solve anything. Taking a deep breath, he turned his back on the brandy and glanced around the room.

The books lining the shelves, the rich wood paneling the walls, even the window glass, painted the picture of gentility and wealth. Yet, the money was only a façade.

Miss Courtney already owned everything else, did she also own him? Did she control his choice of a wife? He ran his fingers through his hair in frustration and tried to think rationally. If he married the spinster, he would gain control of his fortune. A husband controlled his wife's wealth— unless there was a lawyer around to draw up settlement papers keeping the wealth in the woman's name. With his luck, Sir Gerard just knew the solicitor Keller would be the one to interfere.

Aloud, he said, "I will not be forced into marriage."

"Ha!" Linton exclaimed. "Accept your fate and be done with it. Remember what will happen if that money-lender fails to get his blunt back."

Sir Gerard frowned at his friend. "Your reminders are far from helpful." He began to pace through the library, striding from the fireplace to the window, then to the door and around again. "When I choose a wife, she will be of good family."

Linton interrupted. "An heiress is always of good family. This spinster is the daughter of the late vicar, so she is at least genteel."

Without breaking stride, Sir Gerard waved away this comment. "So she is, but she could never be my wife. After being on the fringes of the *ton* for so long, I intend to make my mark upon society. I need a wife who will be an asset to me."

"A meddling spinster as a wife will cause those plans to change."

Halting, Sir Gerard glared at the man still slumped in the chair. "I will not change my plans. I won't. There must be another way to obtain the money. Or at least enough of it to get that man off my back so I can breathe." He cast his glance around the library. "If only I could sell something."

"Can't," Linton pronounced, while staring morosely at the little brandy remaining in his glass. "Everything you own is entailed. She owns everything else."

Sir Gerard was silent, not wanting to admit the truth of that statement. Despairing, he threw himself into one of the wing chairs. "How do other people get money?"

Not realizing it was a rhetorical question, Linton began enumerating on his fingers. "Inheritances, marriages, mortgages, betting . . ."

"I could mortgage the estate." He considered the possibility.

"You are already in debt."

"I would use the rents to pay it off." Sir Gerard's eyes widened, and he leapt to his feet. "That's it! I think I've got it."

Interested at last, Linton straightened in his chair. "What? Got what? Tell me."

"The rents. Why should I even mortgage the estate? Avoid the bankers altogether. I will raise my rents."

The man asked dubiously, "Can you do that?"

"Why not? It's my land." Another thought struck him. "Maybe I will even enclose it for sheep. People are making lots of money in sheep these days."

Even more dubious, Linton raised his eyebrows. "You're going to make your mark in society as a sheep farmer?"

"No, as a gentleman, as Baronet Westcourt." He bowed low. "Now, if you will excuse me, I need to find my steward."

Annette was nervous. Her students seemed to sense it, for restlessness stirred throughout the classroom. One boy tapped his slate in a constant rhythm, while another sought to poke his bench mate whenever Annette glanced away. Her school was beginning with children from four farms, two boys from Mr. Tubbs, and the baker's youngest girl.

She wiped her palms on her skirt and tried to concentrate on the lesson at hand. The chill in the room did not bother her. The trustees would be here at any moment. She wanted to show them her school at its best.

The old warehouse was certainly in better shape. The roof was tight, and the cracks in the walls had been repaired. The old crates and barrel slats were gone. The children sat in rows on new wooden benches, which creaked under their fidgeting. The inadequate stove still needed replacing, but she had a new one ordered. She could make do for now.

In the meantime, Annette was very pleased with the

work of Tubbs the carpenter. He had done his best, plainly remembering several years ago when she had helped his family out when a fever had laid him low. Her baskets of food and clothing, along with some of Sir Nigel's precious coins, had carried him through that bad time.

The clop of horses' hooves and the rattle of carriage wheels outside alerted her to the board's arrival. Every student turned to face the door.

Swallowing, she reminded them, "Children, we must not be distracted from our work."

They obediently bent their heads over their slates again, but their gazes strayed. She pretended not to notice.

The door opened and three men entered. She barely noticed the solicitor and the Reverend Browne as her attention focused on the new baronet. The other men she had known for many years. Because they were familiar with her work, she could trust they would approve of it, even if it took determined convincing on her part. Sir Gerard was the unknown. So far he had plainly shown how much he disapproved of her. For some reason, which she did not want to examine too closely, she wanted his respect for her dream.

"Good afternoon," she greeted the board and led them to the front of the classroom. "As you can see, the children are working very hard on their lessons."

"What are you teaching them?" Mr. Keller asked.

"I plan on reading, writing, and ciphering, but at first, they need to learn their alphabet. Eventually I hope they can read their own Bibles."

The Reverend Browne nodded with pleased appreciation. "An excellent goal."

The trustees gazed around the schoolroom and up at its roof. The vicar said, "Tubbs did excellent work on this warehouse. I wouldn't have thought it possible to repair it so quickly."

"He did indeed," Mr. Keller seconded. "When you first explained your idea for a school, I frankly did not think it could be done. You are a remarkable woman, Miss Courtney."

She smiled at them. "I think Tubbs wanted to help me as thanks for when I had assisted his family."

"Cast your bread upon the waters," the vicar responded.

No longer concerned about the support from the vicar and solicitor, Annette turned to the baronet. He had yet to speak, and his air of concentration concerned her. Unfortunately he examined the stove. From its minute cracks, one could see the hot fire within, but little of its heat warmed the room. Most of the warmth escaped up the piped chimney.

He frowned at her. "You are going to have high heating costs with this stove. It is not adequate for a room of this size."

Naturally the stove would attract him. The one thing she had not yet fixed. She smiled through tight lips. "I have ordered a new one, but it has not yet arrived."

"How long will that take?" he asked. "You could burn quite a bit of coal while waiting."

"Are you concerned about the expense?" she challenged.

"It is one of the duties of a trustee to oversee costs."

"You need not worry, sir. I am covering the charges from my own money."

His jaw tightened. "Perhaps it would have been less costly to wait until everything was in readiness before opening the school."

She stiffened at his criticism, even if there was some

truth to it. He would never approve of her school. As a wastrel, this man probably saw every coin she used as one lost to his gambling.

"Ignorance has held Upper Brampton village in its sway for too long to allow me to wait for the propitious moment." Annette turned back to the other two men. "The children are now writing their letters on their slates. Would you like to see their work?"

If any of the men wanted to groan at the prospect, they were too well-bred to display such ill manners. One by one she introduced each child who approached to display his work. Most of the letters were ragged and ill-formed, except for one student.

"This is Jack. He is the son of Tim and Mary who farm for Hathaway Hall. One of your tenants," she told Sir Gerard.

"I recognize Jack," the vicar said. He beamed at the boy of about eleven years with the raggedly trimmed brown hair and sharp nose. "Are you working hard, son?"

"Yes, sir."

The lad handed over his slate to the baronet. It displayed evenly written letters in a clear hand.

"Why, this is quite neat!" the Reverend Browne exclaimed. "You are doing very well."

"Thank you, sir."

Annette said, "If he keeps on improving the way he is, I think he will be able to serve as a clerk someday." She cast a hopeful glance at the solicitor as she spoke, but he appeared to be studying the rafters.

Sir Gerard handed the slate back to the boy. "How long have you been working on these letters, Jack?"

"Only since the school opened this week, sir," the boy replied.

The baronet nodded at the response, but did not speak further. Jack's speed at his studies pleased Annette, and she was glad she could already display an early positive result of her school. Maybe then Sir Gerard would drop his opposition.

The rest of the inspection went quickly. Mr. Keller and the Reverend Browne praised her work and that of the children, yet she did not hear anything from the baronet.

As she escorted them to the door, she asked Sir Gerard, "Are you pleased with the school?" And tried not to let her hopes rise before he answered.

He paused during his exit and studied her. She met his gaze directly, but inwardly her heart raced. He did not like her, but would the dislike extend to her work? If he supported it, then her dream would be justified, despite the expense.

He answered in a slow, deep voice. "I agree with the other men, you are a remarkable woman, Miss Courtney. This school is off to a good start. There is order here, and it was inexpensively done."

A gratified feeling began to seep through her until he continued, "I will set aside a sum from my uncle's fortune to administer it in the future."

She stared in disbelief. "Your uncle's wealth is already funding the school."

"For now."

The solicitor intervened, "Now, see here—"

Annette's clipped farewell interrupted. "Thank you, gentlemen, for visiting *my* school. I am glad you endorse my work."

"Except for the stove," Sir Gerard reminded her.

She glared at him. "I promise there will be a new stove here by your next visit."

He bowed and left with the other men. She shut the door behind them and leaned against it. Her students watched her avidly, no longer making a pretense of working. With such dramatics playing, she did not blame them.

However, she needed time to think, so she gave them the first command that occurred to her. "Finish writing your alphabet neatly."

With her back against the door, she wondered why Sir Gerard's approval held such importance to her. He made very plain his only interest in her was caused by the inheritance. No dance at the Assembly could disguise the fact.

Yet, his approval of her school pleased her, even if it was qualified. *I am spending the money wisely*, she told herself. *It is not being frittered away. Why, I have used it to repair the church's roof and to start this school. And I have done it carefully, too.*

She nodded to herself for emphasis. Only the stove remained to bother her. She would take care of that detail right now.

"Children, school is dismissed for the day." Above the instant noise for departure, she added, "Because you did so well during the inspection, I will treat you to candy at the store."

Shrill whistles and loud cheers met this announcement, and she smiled. In no time, she led the children like a happy flock of chattering chicks to the merchant. They noisily selected their treats before dashing home.

"Put the candy on my account," she instructed the shopkeeper.

"Certainly, Miss Courtney."

"I also wanted to check as to when the stove will arrive for the school."

"It should take another week or so," he answered. "The

winter roads are in a sad state this time of the year, making deliveries difficult."

She nodded. The answer did not surprise her. It was February. Although it would be expensive to continue using the old stove, she could not afford to let the wintertime pass without her school. Once the weather turned, the children would be required to help with the farm work. She must give them as much education as she could before that happened.

"Miss Courtney, will there be anything else you need today?" the man asked.

"I will take some of that candy for Lucille."

"Certainly. I'll wrap it." While he busied himself with the paper and string, he said, "It is a pleasure doing business with you."

"Thank you," she replied politely. Since she had inherited the money, all the local merchants found pleasure in her business.

When Annette headed back to her cottage with the candy package in her hand, she assured herself she was well satisfied with the day. Even if that baronet did not want to acknowledge it, he had to admit her school was doing well. Filled with determined righteousness, she declared, "I know how to handle the money. Now I need to consider the next project."

Posture held upright, she tramped home along the wet lane and never noticed she did not claim the fortune as *her* money.

Chapter Seven

Annette anticipated that spring farm chores would interfere with her school's attendance. However, when for the third day in a row, only five students appeared, she knew something was wrong. This was only the third week of February, for goodness' sake. The weather was wet and cold and muddy. Too early for spring planting.

She called Jack to her. "Do you know why the others are not here?"

"Yes, ma'am." He shuffled his feet, while she waited patiently. "They must work, ma'am."

"Work? At what? Spring planting is weeks away."

More feet shuffling. He had washed his face and hands before coming, and his hair was combed but still ragged. "I don't right know what, ma'am."

Annette took pity on his obvious reluctance. "You don't need to be afraid to tell me," she said gently. "I cannot help if I do not know what the difficulty is."

"I don't know what they're working on," Jack burst out. "I couldn't think of anything to do so I came to school."

The words echoed in the almost empty room. She overlooked the implication that school was his last resort. Something was seriously amiss. Placing her arm about his shoulders, she asked, "Why do you need to do anything? What is wrong? Is there sickness?" If so, it would be odd that no one had yet come to her for assistance.

"No, no sickness. It's the rents."

"The rents?"

"They've gone up."

Annette wasted no time debating the fact. "How much?"

He seemed more at ease now that the news was out. "A lot. Me pa owes an extra ten pounds—by March quarter end. Where is he going to get so much money so fast?"

"Ten pounds? In addition to the regular rent?"

Jack nodded.

"That's outrageous!" Her arm dropped from his shoulder, and she sputtered with indignation. "I expected some changes, but not this!"

"Then you can do something?" Hope lit Jack's thin face. The other students also gazed at her as if torn between hope and fear.

She asked them, "Are your families also facing such steep increases in their rents?"

They nodded.

She knew they understood her concern for them. "And the children who are not here, are their rents also raised?"

"Yes, ma'am," Jack answered.

"There must be a mistake." Annette squared her shoulders. "I will speak to the baronet about this."

"Will speaking do any good?" The boy appeared to have become the spokesman for the class.

"My words will because this mistake will be cleared

up," she promised. She patted him on the back as she sent him back to his seat on the bench.

Within her burned the need to confront Sir Gerard immediately. Obviously there was something wrong, some error committed. It was her duty to correct it.

Perhaps he meant to raise the rent by ten pounds over the year and somehow it was reported as per quarter. With prices so high due to the war on the Continent, even an additional pound every three months would be a hardship to Jack's parents. The other tenants faced the same difficulties. She must make the baronet understand how impossible his intentions were. As soon as she dismissed the school, she planned to do just that.

The stables at Hathaway Hall continued to have the power to attract the baronet. The memory of Nat the groom hung over the familiar stalls, along with the air dusty from the straw and heavy with the earthy smell of horses. Remembering the acceptance he had found here, Sir Gerard felt at ease in the rustic surroundings.

He brushed his stallion's smooth gray coat. Beneath his hands, he felt the strong muscles bunch and relax. Silver Shadow tossed his head, shaking the white mane his master had just combed.

"Does it feel good, old fellow?" He rubbed the bristles of the brush behind Silver Shadow's ear.

The horse snorted in response. Smiling, the baronet resumed his task. Taking care of his horse was one of the small joys in his life. He lived in the social world of the *haute ton*, but he was equally at home in the simple world of the stable. After all, Silver Shadow had always accepted him without judgmental reproach.

Behind him, he heard a splash as someone crossed the

stable yard. Turning, he saw the money-lender, Mortimer Wallace, picking his way passed the puddles.

Surprised, Sir Gerard exclaimed, "What are you doing here?"

Wallace smoothed his jacket. "Surely you should have expected me. This is February, after all."

Although he knew what was coming, Sir Gerard turned back to his horse. "I am aware of the date. I just did not expect to see you here."

"I called at your house, but I became tired of waiting." The man's voice remained full and rich, but an edge underlay the tone. "You cannot avoid me."

"I am not avoiding you." The rhythmic brush strokes helped him keep his temper, and his fear, at bay.

"Excellent," Wallace oozed. "Then you can repay my loan now."

"I only owe you an installment."

"I want the full amount."

"I will pay only what I owe. Nothing more."

Sir Gerard felt the money-lender's eyes boring into his back. Beneath his master's less certain touch, Silver Shadow moved restlessly. He tried to calm the horse with soothing words, but he kept his ears tuned for Wallace's next words.

"*Could* you pay me the installment due now?" the other man asked.

"Of course," Sir Gerard lied.

"Then I will be happy to take it in my hands and leave you."

The baronet paused in his brushing and faced the urbane financier. "Do you think I keep such a sum on me in the stables?"

Wallace smiled. There was no sincerity in the upturn of

his muscles. "Of course not. I will walk with you back to the strongbox in your house."

Knowing very well that the box was empty, Sir Gerard shrugged. "Nor do I keep such a sum in my house. I do not intend to tempt thieves."

The smile shrank a little. "Then I will accept a draft on your bank. In fact, you should have sent one to me already. I dislike having to collect it myself. This is a task more appropriate for underlings."

Inwardly Sir Gerard relaxed slightly. Without realizing it, Wallace had tacitly accepted the installment payment rather than the full repayment of the loan. Not that he could even pay the smaller sum.

"Then send your underlings."

"I am here, and I will collect your draft." The smile definitely had vanished from the man's round face.

"Later." Sir Gerard resumed his brushing, moving down one of the forelegs.

"That draft was due to me at the end of January. It is now the third week of February, and I want my money— now."

The baronet heard the implicit threat. Linton had told him of the physical problems that overtook those already burdened with financial difficulties from Wallace. A saddle cinch cut. The wheel of a carriage loosened. Footpads attacking. Misfortunes that could happen to anyone, seemed to happen to unfortunate clients of the moneylender. Even knowing the whispers of what happened to those who could not repay, there was nothing Sir Gerard could do.

Pretending a nonchalance he was far from feeling, he picked up the horse's leg and inspected the hoof. He used the brush to wipe away the dried mud from the morning's ride.

Apparently his attitude annoyed Wallace, for anger burned through his next words. "You owe me that money, sir, and I have every right to expect repayment. Those who gamble at the tables must satisfy their debts of honor. Isn't that what you told me when you came to me for help?"

"Yes, it was," Sir Gerard replied.

"You also told me you had inherited your uncle's fortune."

"I was his heir!" He stood and faced his tormentor. "And you were familiar with the extent of that fortune."

"It is my business to know such things."

"You certainly did not know that he willed the bulk of it away."

With a wave of his hand, Wallace airily dismissed his statement. "An error on my part. Don't compound the error by welshing on your debt to me. *You* may not consider it a debt of honor, but *I* consider my repayment to be as important as any debt to a gentleman. Actually it is more important because it is owed to me."

Sir Gerard stared at the man. How could he escape this situation? There was no way to get rid of Wallace because there was no money to buy his departure.

At that moment a woman rounded the corner of the house and headed to the stables. With a groan, Sir Gerard realized it was Miss Courtney. He did not need her presence adding to his troubles.

Unlike the money-lender, she did not mince her way across the stable yard. She headed straight for him with determination, stepping across the puddles without breaking her stride. Naturally, she did not slip in the mud.

"Sir Gerard," she called. "I need to speak with you immediately."

"I can meet with you in the house as soon as I have cleaned up," he offered.

"This cannot wait." She arrived at the stable doorway and cast a dismissing glance at Wallace that caused Sir Gerard to smile. He did not think the man was used to being considered unimportant.

"It seems I have turned my stable into my drawing room, since I am receiving all of my callers here," he commented.

The money-lender's gaze frankly assessed the spinster. Sir Gerard wagered to himself that she puzzled the man. She wore the serviceable brown dress and severe hairstyle of a companion, yet she comported herself as if she were of a higher rank.

She said, "There has been a dreadful mistake made which needs to be cleared up now."

At her determination, Sir Gerard seized the opportunity to dismiss Wallace. "I have said all I intend on this matter. You may go."

Wallace's nostrils flared. "You don't get rid of me so easily. This is not over between us."

With another assessing glance at Miss Courtney, he stepped around the stable's corner and out of sight.

Relieved to have that difficulty sent off, Sir Gerard patiently turned to his caller. "What is wrong, Miss Courtney?"

She wasted no words in her explanation. "The rents have been raised. The tenants believe they owe much more than they should at the end of this quarter. You must correct this error."

For a moment he studied her. Her gaze was so direct

and clear that she plainly assumed he was in agreement with her. A sense of remorse flashed through him, yet immediately after Wallace's demands, he could not yield to it. "What makes you think the tenants are mistaken?"

Her eyes widened in horrified surprise. "You cannot mean to place such a burden upon your people! It is too oppressive!"

Unable to face her, he returned to his brushing of Silver Shadow, redoing the flanks he had already done. "I need that money."

"Please, you must reconsider. This is too much!"

The remorse weighed heavily upon his heart. He knew she was right. The extra rent would be an impossible burden for his tenants. Yet, he also knew not repaying Wallace endangered his own safety. He did not respond to her plea and returned to his brushing.

Watching him, his air of disinterest bewildered her. Annette was certain he cared for the welfare of his people. "Sir Gerard, why are you raising these rents?"

"I told you I needed the money."

She heard the defeat in his voice, and her own manner gentled. There was some problem here of which she was not aware. Perhaps she could help. "So you said, but not why."

Someone cleared his throat, interrupting them. Turning, she saw the large man had not left the stables, only hidden out of sight in order to eavesdrop. Now he had revealed himself. She frowned at his despicable behavior.

"Avoiding a problem again, Sir Gerard?" A sneer crossed the man's face. "Perhaps I can help you, ma'am." He offered her his card.

Annette took it. "Financier?" she read.

"Yes. I assist those who have monetary troubles."

She remained puzzled.

He explained further, "I make loans. If money causes you problems, I can help you."

"For a price," Sir Gerard interposed bitterly. "You are barking up the wrong tree with her, Wallace. Miss Courtney does not have 'monetary troubles.' She is the woman who inherited my uncle's fortune."

"Indeed!" His eyes gleamed, and he pasted an ingratiating smile on his face. He bowed low. "I am very pleased to make your acquaintance, Miss Courtney. Perhaps I can interest you in some investment projects of mine."

"I am not interested in discussing investments now," she said.

Wallace glanced between her and Sir Gerard. The baronet had stopped grooming his horse and stood impassively, resting his hand on the animal's back.

"I fancy I can explain the baronet's difficulty." She heard the mocking laughter in his voice and disliked him. Still, she listened to what he said. "He owes me money, a lot of it. I'll bet he raised the tenants' rents to repay me."

She looked at the baronet with a question in her eyes. He set down the brush and faced her. "It's true," he told her quietly.

"I only wonder, Sir Gerard," Wallace continued, "since the rents aren't due until the end of March, how were you going to meet your payment past due since the end of January?"

"I would have delayed you somehow."

Wallace stiffened. "I do not like delayed payments. Surely my reputation warned you of that."

The baronet ignored him. Instead, he gazed upon Annette. "I am sorry about the tenants. I was so caught in my own problems that I did not think about the hardship I was imposing."

She read sincerity in his dark brown eyes. "What are you going to do?"

A half smile twisted his lips. "I will rescind the rent increase."

"What about you?" she asked.

Wallace interposed. "Yes, what about my money?"

"I will think of something."

"You are already past due," the money-lender reminded him with menace in his voice.

"I know that."

"I will pay it," Annette said.

"What!" Both men stared at her in astonishment.

She, too, was astonished at her words. Why she had come to Sir Gerard's rescue, Annette did not know. Maybe it was because she always wanted to solve problems. Now was not the time to ponder her reasons.

With firmness in her voice, she repeated, "I will pay it. How much is the payment?"

"Miss Courtney, I cannot let you do this!" Sir Gerard exclaimed.

Wallace rubbed his hands together. "You are a most generous woman, Miss Courtney."

She ignored his flattery. "What is the payment amount?"

"Miss Courtney, these are my debts. They were debts of honor. I incurred them, and I borrowed the funds to repay them. You cannot pay them for me."

She lifted her eyebrows at him. "Betting, Sir Gerard?"

"Yes, if it matters."

"It only matters if you do not oppress your people to repay them."

His lips curled. "You always have the right answer, don't you, Miss Courtney?"

"In this case, I also happen to have the money," she replied. There was a tightness about her chest as if her lungs were clamped in a carpenter's vise. Sadness overlay her soul. It hurt to realize he was the wastrel his uncle had named him, but practicalities summoned her attention.

She turned to the money-lender. With her back to the baronet, she arranged to send Wallace to the solicitor's office for the draft of the payment owed.

"Thank you, Miss Courtney. It has been a pleasure doing business with you." Wallace bowed low in farewell to her. Then he strolled away, obviously well pleased with himself.

"I hope I need never encounter that unpleasant man again," Annette said, watching him go to make certain he truly departed.

In the ensuing silence, Silver Shadow stamped his hoof, as if recalling his master to the grooming that was not finished.

"I will pay you back," Sir Gerard promised.

"I expect you to do so." She looked him straight in the face. "But not on the backs of your tenants. Those rent increases must be dropped."

He nodded. "They will be. I can live on the regular quarter rents."

"And repay me?"

His fingers played with the horse's mane. "Yes. It just will not be the life I expected as Baronet Westcourt."

She bit back the words, telling him that life seldom was lived as expected. Her purpose was accomplished; she did not need to moralize to him. "Shall I spread the word that the rents will not be increased?"

"I will do it."

"The news will ease their worries."

His voice was quiet. "You are quite the ministering angel, aren't you, Miss Courtney?"

"I only try to do what is right." Although never before had duty brought with it such a sense of dragging disappointment. She shook herself free from her melancholy thoughts. "Thank you for reducing the rents. I must leave to instruct Mr. Keller to write that draft."

"Actually, it is I who thank you—from the bottom of my heart."

The sincerity and embarrassed gratitude she heard in his voice tugged at her heart. He stood before her with one hand resting on his horse's back. His white shirt was open at the neck, and bits of straw clung to his knees. Even with his hair in disarray, he was a well-favored man in appearance. But only in looks. Today's encounter showed he was, in fact, a wastrel.

With a deepening sense of disappointment, she wrenched her gaze away from him and hurried out into the stable yard, heading for home. At her speed, the ruts in the road staggered her balance, but she pressed on. She had kept searching and searching for proof that the baronet was the profligate his uncle had named him, and now she had found it. The fact brought her no joy.

A money-lender. That was what Wallace was despite calling himself a financier. Further, Sir Gerard's gambling had brought him into the man's clutches.

The baronet was a very clever man, Annette had to grant him that. He disguised his proclivity well. Although she had watched sharply, she had never spotted him at the Assembly card rooms nor heard a whisper of any bets placed by him in Upper Brampton village.

She had even begun to believe Sir Nigel had wronged his nephew. No longer! Her eyes were opened. Sir Nigel had done the right thing when he bequeathed the fortune to her. She shuddered at how it would have been wasted in his nephew's hands.

She must never let him get his hands on it. She knew her duty.

Chapter Eight

The feeling of relief, of disaster averted, still pervaded Sir Gerard the next morning. He knew his debt to the money-lender continued to be owed, yet such a heavy weight of worry had lifted that the sharp edge of reality was banished to the boundaries of fantasy. He now had the luxury of time.

Out for his morning ride, he felt truly master of his future. That the future remained uncertain did not encroach upon his light heart. With exhilaration he raced Silver Shadow down the roads, periodically whooping just to hear his voice among the trees and across the meadows.

Then he leisurely dined alone at a late breakfast, exuding goodwill toward the world in general. Linton had left after requesting the use of the carriage. Sir Gerard presumed he meant to call upon some of the neighbors, but he did not concern himself overmuch about it.

The butler entered with a card upon his silver salver. "A man here to see you, sir."

Sir Gerard had the first inkling of trouble at the sight of that white paper and at Newton's lack of reference to a gentleman. He picked up the card. Mortimer Wallace, financier. Instantly his pleasant illusions shattered before living reality. He would have to receive the man.

Setting down his suddenly tasteless jam-covered toast, he asked, "Where is he?"

"I put him in the drawing room, sir."

This time when Sir Gerard entered the formal receiving room, he noticed the money-lender had not made himself at home. Instead, the man stood in the center of the Oriental rug, impatiently tapping a walking stick against his leg.

"I am surprised to see you here," Sir Gerard said. "I thought our business was settled."

"Yes, the spinster paid the first installment of your loan, but you still owe the balance."

A chill filled Sir Gerard. "I am aware of that."

"Are you aware that it is the full amount which is due?"

"The payment was made!" Sir Gerard exclaimed. "The next one is not due until the end of February."

Wallace stopped tapping his stick. "I see I was wise to stop here on my way back to London. You are under a serious misapprehension, sir."

One eyebrow raised in silent question as inwardly Sir Gerard waited for the blow to fall. "Explain yourself."

"Indeed." Wallace nodded slightly. "When I last visited you, I told you the whole loan amount was due."

"That was only because you feared the first payment would be missed."

"It *was* missed. It was late by a couple of weeks." The man shook his head. "I cannot allow such delays in my business. Time is money."

Sir Gerard kept his temper in check. Through clenched teeth, he said, "I regret the wait."

"I do, too. I am calling the entire loan due. You are too great of a credit risk for me."

"What? How can I pay off the entire amount now? You know it is impossible!"

"I admit you just made a payment on your account, and I am willing to be a reasonable man." He paused to study the tip of his walking stick. "I will agree to allow you a two-week extension from today to repay me the balance."

"Only two weeks!"

Wallace looked up directly into Sir Gerard's eyes. The baronet nearly stepped backwards at the coldness in the man's gaze. No mercy or understanding flickered in those dark depths. In their lack of humanity, the man's glare reminded him of the unblinking stare of a snake.

"Yes, two weeks," the money-lender repeated. "It would be wise of you, Sir Gerard, if your payment was not late again. I dislike being required to remind debtors of what is owed. It can become quite . . . physical."

With that warning, Wallace bowed and left, leaving Sir Gerard standing in stunned dismay. His breakfast toast weighed heavily in his stomach. With stiff, jerky movements he made his way to a chair and sank into it. He stared out the window at the broad expanse of lawn surrounding Hathaway Hall. Unlike earlier this morning, the sight did not raise his spirits.

His spirits and his future were both shipwrecked. He could not pay the balance. Not in two weeks. Not even in a month. Perhaps with careful managing, he could pay his debt off according to the original agreed upon schedule. But not in two weeks.

He ran his hands through his hair, trying to think of what to do. Briefly he considered the card tables. He had about five pounds upstairs. It would barely provide one stake. If the cards were not dealt in his favor, he would have nothing left. But still the chance tempted him. Could he parlay five pounds into the seven hundred and fifty he owed within two weeks?

He doubted it, but he would try. And he would continue his campaign to regain his fortune.

Annette found the weekly Wednesday night Assemblies to be far more enjoyable than ever before. She liked the attention paid to her. She liked having a partner for every dance. She even liked wearing the pretty gowns Lucille had insisted upon.

She would not admit, to herself or anyone else, that she liked meeting Baronet Westcourt. Somehow, the evening never sparkled until she spotted his arrival. He seldom missed a week.

Tonight she kept a sharp eye out for him, but without the same sense of breathless anticipation as last week. After the meeting with the money-lender yesterday afternoon, disillusionment weighed her down. She had begun to believe Sir Nigel wrong about his nephew. The old miser had not been a pleasant person, and she had started to like the new heir.

But it appeared the uncle had correctly named Sir Gerard a wastrel.

She flinched at the memory of her realization in the stable. Determined to put it behind her, she plied her fan vigorously and attempted to pay attention to her partner's conversation.

Until she spotted Sir Gerard.

He must have just arrived, for his friend Mr. Robert Linton was still by his side, not yet caught up in the gaiety of the dances. Now that her eyes were opened to Sir

Gerard's true nature, she studied him, looking for those signs of dissipation her previous examinations apparently overlooked.

The baronet appeared magnificent in his London-tailored evening clothes. The black coat and white shirt with its intricate cravat showed none of the wear she would have expected a wastrel to need to conceal. Certainly such a man would not be able to afford to keep up the evening style Sir Gerard displayed. His debts would be too high. Of course, there was always the money-lender.

She sighed, wishing the picture thus presented were the true man and not a façade.

Her partner, Mr. Alfred Deschamps, mistook her sigh. "I knew your tender heart could not resist the appeal of my four children who so need a mother. In fact, I always admired your devotion to your own invalid mother. It showed how strongly you do your duty."

With a start, Annette realized this was the prelude to another marriage proposal. Where once she had longed for even one offer, the current inundation now wearied her. "Speak no further, Mr. Deschamps," she said, tapping her fan on his lips to halt the flow of words. Lately she had become quite practiced at these flirtation techniques. Except she did not care about coquetry and removed the fan.

"But you have not heard what I have to say—"

To herself she thought, *I have already heard every other man say it.* Aloud, she said, "I will not be able to give you the answer you seek."

Mr. Alfred Deschamps tugged at his graying sideburns. "Is there someone else? I heard no mention of any interest."

Annette took no offense at the fact that her life was a

subject of the local gossip mongering. She had lived in Upper Brampton too long not to know discussion of others' doings was one of the chief entertainments. Lately, her life must have provided much grist for the mill.

"No, there is no one else," she told him. Yet her eyes strayed involuntarily towards where the baronet still stood.

His gaze was focused in the direction of the card room. A sense of trepidation filled Annette. More debt could cause the rents to be raised. She could not be forever rescuing him from the consequences of his folly, or else she might as well hand the whole fortune over to him at once instead of doling it out piecemeal.

With a hastily polite farewell to Mr. Deschamps, Annette disengaged herself from his attentions and headed towards Sir Gerard. With his brows drawn together, a look of concentration filled his face. He directed his gaze towards the card room and did not notice her bearing down upon him.

Mr. Robert Linton did. He stepped forward to greet Annette. "Good evening, Miss Courtney. I am so pleased to see you. If this dance is free, I would like to be your partner."

She feared the direction of the baronet's look and resolved to thwart his plans. "Actually, I had saved it for your friend."

Taken aback, Linton blinked. "I say. Perhaps then you'll join me for a carriage ride tomorrow?"

The request was obviously the first thing that had popped into his head, but Annette did not care. "Certainly, Mr. Linton. I would enjoy it." She waited expectantly for the baronet to speak.

Linton nudged him. With a start, Sir Gerard suddenly

seemed to become aware of her presence and bowed in greeting. "Good evening, Miss Courtney."

She smiled as she curtsied in response.

"Aren't you going to ask her to dance?" Linton suggested.

Sir Gerard cast a quick glance at the card room before offering her his arm. "Of course, I am. May I have the honor of this dance?"

Her smile became fixed as determination filled her. He was not going to play cards that evening. "Certainly, sir."

She placed her hand upon his arm and joined him in the dance. It was a set of lively country dances. Temporarily she forgot his intentions as she gave herself up to partnering a masterful dancer. He never missed a step. If she momentarily stumbled, he smoothly caught her up and kept the rhythm of the dance unabated. Yet, his confidence increased her own. Her mistakes became few, and she matched him step for step. When he grinned at her, she smiled back, ready to laugh at any quip he might speak, but the pace of the dance was too fast for conversation.

All too soon the music ended, and the merriment she felt towards him dispersed. She remembered her purpose.

Fortunately, the lively country dance gave veracity to Annette's breathless request to sit the next one out. Sir Gerard led her to a small alcove where they could speak privately.

Once they were seated, he eyed her with one brow raised. "Now that we are private, perhaps you would wish to tell me what is on your mind."

His directness startled her and then pleased her. She preferred the open approach. "Because of yesterday, I feared you might be tempted into the card room."

His lips curved. "You intended, therefore, to save me from myself?"

This speech was more direct than she expected from him, but Annette responded to it. "Yes, I did."

"Have you ever seen me gambling, Miss Courtney?"

"No, but I remember what Sir Nigel said."

Sir Gerard reminded her, "My uncle was not the most accurate judge of character."

"True, but then I met the money-lender."

He stiffened. The last of the camaraderie she felt with him during the dance disappeared. "Wallace's presence changed everything, didn't it?"

"He is evidence that is hard to overlook," she acknowledged carefully.

"Were you looking for evidence?"

Now it was her turn to shift uncomfortably on her chair. "I did not want to find it."

Briefly he studied her. She forced herself to meet his gaze. What he sought from her, she did not know. She had not wanted to find the wastrel in a man she had begun to admire. It hurt to find the flaw.

"Now that you believe my uncle's assessment, what would you have me do?"

She leaned forward and grasped his arm, hardly aware of doing so, until she felt its firmness beneath her fingers. The strength he had so recently used to guide her on the dance floor. A strength not gained through hours of card playing. Again he confused her, but she clung to her purpose.

"Do not go into the card room," she begged. "Do not bet again. You will only end up in that money-lender's clutches again."

Making no move to withdraw his arm, he asked, "Since

you believe me to be a wastrel, why does it bother you so if I gamble?"

"Because your gambling affects more than you. The money you spend is earned by the labor of your tenants."

"Yet it is *my* money."

"It would be better spent on your estate. For instance, the cottages of your tenants are nearly in ruins. Sir Nigel never kept them up."

"I am well aware that my uncle never spent a farthing unless it worked for his own comfort or wealth. Remember, I lived with the man."

"Then you will forgo the card room tonight?"

Smiling, he placed his hand over hers. She felt its warmth through her glove, and a glow spread to her heart and down to her toes.

"I will not seek the card room," he promised. "But what would you have me do instead?"

"Dance?" she suggested.

"Why, Miss Courtney, how forward of you!"

For one of the first times in her life, she felt the heat of a blush radiate from her cheeks.

"I did not mean with me," she mumbled. Then she spotted the teasing amusement in his eyes.

Standing, he bowed before her. "I would love to dance this next set with you—or do you think the ladies of the village would gossip avidly if you partnered me twice in a row?"

To her surprise, she found she did want to dance with him again. Despite her interference in his life, he had listened to her. She was used to men denouncing her as a meddling old maid, along with other terms. But Baronet Westcourt had agreed with her. She felt greatly in charity towards him. Besides, lately her life had done nothing but provide entertainment for the gossips of Upper Brampton.

"I would love to dance with you," she told him.

During tea the next afternoon, Annette and Lucille discussed the previous night's Assembly.

"He wanted to gamble in that card room," Annette said, "but I just could not allow it."

Lucille shook her head in dismay. "It's that money-lender's fault."

"I wish you were right, but no, he was only trying to collect the money due to him. I fear Sir Gerard is the wastrel his uncle declared."

Sipping her tea, Lucille thought a moment. "You know, Annette, betting is not frowned upon among his class."

"I believe a gentleman always pays his debts of honor first to those of his own class. It is the tradesmen who are delayed and thus suffer." She reached for one of the cakes arranged on the tray. Their cottage now possessed the luxuries of a cook and a maid.

"Sir Gerard must have always paid what he owed, or else he wouldn't still be accepted by society," the other woman pointed out.

"Where on earth would he obtain the funds to bet? Not from Sir Nigel. That must be how he met with the money-lender."

A slight knock announced the arrival of the maid. "Mr. Linton is here."

With a startled gasp, Annette hastily set her cup down. "Oh, dear! I forgot I promised to ride in his carriage today."

Lucille ran a quick assessing look over her friend's wardrobe. "Thank goodness you are not wearing one of those ugly brown dresses. That dark green will do very well to receive him." To the maid she said, "Please show him in."

Annette cast a fulminating glance at her companion, but could not respond further, since Mr. Linton entered the room. He wore a dark wool coat tailored to show him to an advantage. However, as she stood to greet him, she could not stop the brief thought that expert tailoring displayed better on the baronet.

After greetings, Mr. Linton asked her, "Are you ready?"

"Just let me get my coat and bonnet," she said.

"The day is cool but the sun is warm. Also there is no wind," he informed her. "It is a fine day for a drive."

"I look forward to it."

Very shortly, they were tooling down the road outside the village. Annette savored the brisk air in her lungs, but kept her hands warm inside her fur muff. It had been several days since any fresh snow had fallen. None remained on the bare branches, but wide patches of it lay off the road beneath the trees. Little traffic was out despite being late afternoon, so Mr. Linton's skills as a driver were not in demand. Instead, they passed the drive in conversation.

"Sir Gerard is my best friend," Linton said. "That's why I came with him when his uncle died."

"Your deed bespeaks a generous heart," Annette replied.

He snorted. "I'm not the one who expected to be generous. I thought Sir Gerard could help me out with my financial difficulties."

"Gambling?"

"You needn't freeze up on me that way, Miss Courtney. Betting is fun."

"Not when you bet more than you can afford."

"But that is how men like Sir Gerard and me survive in this world."

"Through gambling and debts?" Her assessment of the baronet's character and that of his friends was getting worse and worse.

Guiding the horse, Linton shook his head. "It's not the way you think."

Since she did not intend to leap from the moving carriage to escape the taint of his apparent wickedness, she said, "Why don't you explain it to me, then?"

"We live by our wits and the social round. There is no other place for us in society."

Annette mulled this statement over as the horse clip-clopped along the wet lane. "I am afraid I still don't understand."

"Society is based upon expectations. It is not only who you are, but whom you will become. Me, I don't have much in the way of expectations. I am the younger son of a younger son. There's not much open to me."

"Nonsense, Mr. Linton. You and I both know that many younger sons make their way in this world through the church, the army, or the law."

He gave a dry laugh devoid of humor. "Do you think I haven't considered those paths? I am not army mad. I like my creature comforts too much, thank you. Nor am I devout enough for the church."

Despite the example of her father, Annette privately agreed that too many of the clergy did not properly lead their flocks. "There remains the law."

His hoarse laugh grated on her nerves. "The law! Somehow I cannot picture myself locked away in a musty old office like your solicitor."

"Mr. Keller is a very fine man," she defended. "And he has helped me greatly."

"Only because you have the money."

Although she disliked his assessment, she privately agreed that it was probably true and dropped her defense.

He continued, "Money and title determine your place in society. I have neither, but Sir Gerard had the expectations of inheriting both when his uncle died."

"It seems a morbid way to live," she remarked. "Spending your whole life waiting for another's death."

He shrugged. "It's the way life is. Sir Gerard used his expectations to support himself. The prospective title of baronet was real enough to society, but he had no allowance to enable him to live among the *ton* as he deserved."

Annette thought of the baronet's fine clothes, exquisite manners, and magnificent horse. "I am not sure any amount of allowance would have enabled him to live at the standard he preferred. Just look at his clothes and his horse."

"Oh, no, Miss Courtney, you wrong him!" In his earnestness, Mr. Linton loosened the reins, and immediately the horse began to slow. "The clothes and his horse are all that Sir Gerard owns. He earned the horse when a colt in exchange for some training he provided. He could not bear to sell him, despite the price he would bring. The clothes he needs to go about in society."

Shocked, Annette asked, "You mean he has no money of his own?"

"During the Season, he lives by the social round with its dinners and dances, which is why the clothes are so important. At other times he is invited to different country estates where he will help train the owner's horses—but only in a gentlemanly fashion, you understand. He raised Silver Shadow to be the horse he is today."

Annette sank back against the seat, her mind in a whirl. At last she was beginning to comprehend Sir Gerard's position. "No wonder he wants the fortune so badly."

Linton's face brightened. "Does that mean you will now give it to him?"

She glanced sharply at him. Linton freely proclaimed himself the baronet's friend. Perhaps this tale was only invented to gain her sympathy. Yet, it had the ring of truth. "If Sir Gerard needed money to live on so desperately that he must sponge off others, why did he never visit his uncle?"

"What makes you think he was welcome at Hathaway Hall?" Linton slapped the reins across the horse's back. "You knew the old baronet, Miss Courtney. Would he have taken his nephew in?"

She remembered the thundering lectures about the "wastrel" she had been forced to endure. "His duty . . ." she began, but both her voice and argument were weak. She knew Sir Nigel had cared not a fig about his duty. Not to his nephew and not to his tenants. Only her constant persistence had gained the meager amounts she had wrested from him.

Linton continued on as if he had not heard her. "We both attended Cambridge, but I lasted longer. When Sir Gerard was sent down from school, he did not even bother to head for Upper Brampton village. There was nothing for him at Hathaway Hall. Instead, he went to London where he quickly learned the social skills necessary to survive. Eventually, I followed him."

Having experienced Sir Gerard's social abilities for herself, Annette knew how well he could charm. Somehow she never thought of proper deportment as a means of support. To her, manners were something a civilized person lived to make life beautiful and serene, not for financial reasons.

Linton's revelations about his friend's life confused her. The way of life he described sounded wrong, but she, too, had suffered from the meanness of Sir Nigel's character. How much worse life must have been for a boy growing up under his care! She shuddered at the picture. The past should not excuse Sir Gerard's way of life, but she understood what drove him to it.

She laid a hand gently on Linton's arm. "Thank you for telling me about the baronet's past."

He glanced at her arm and grinned. "I don't suppose you would be interested in marrying me? I am not considered too demanding a fellow by my friends."

Knowing his heart was not in the proposal, she laughed. "No, I fear I must decline your offer. I think you are looking more for a steady allowance than a wife."

"Sometimes the only way to get that allowance is with a wife," he retorted, but the grin remained on his face.

In that lighthearted mood, the drive ended. Yet even during the next day's school lessons, Annette continued to ponder what she had learned. Had Sir Nigel willed away the money as a final infliction of spite upon his nephew? She had never comprehended why she was chosen. Perhaps she was only an instrument of vindictiveness. She disliked that prospect.

No matter what the reason, she had inherited. Looking around the schoolroom at the children industriously scratching on their slates, she knew she used the wealth to good purpose. These children were hers. Not of her body, but of her longing.

Jack quickly asserted his abilities, and now she regarded him as her prize student. He was the son of one of the baronet's tenant farmers, yet he displayed an aptitude for learning that secretly astonished her. Far sooner than she had expected, she would have to do something about finding a position for him. Her heart swelled with pride at discovering such riches in her student.

Little Molly sat on a bench in front of Jack. She was the baker's daughter. Her laborious movements on the slate were not as certain as the boy's, but her tongue sticking out between her teeth indicated her determination. When the girl glanced up, Annette smiled with encouragement.

Although different from Sir Gerard's, these children had hard lives, too. He had faced enmity from the one who should have offered a home. Her students faced physical hardship and sometimes abuse, but none of them were actively hated by those who were charged to care for them. Which was worse, to be an inconvenient child or one who was actively hated?

She knew they eagerly waited her ringing of the dismissal bell, and then they would tear off for their homes. For just a moment, she delayed and savored the feeling that they were her family.

"That is all for today," she announced, and she clanged the dismissal bell.

Immediately the chatter and clatter of children resounded in the building. Reveling, Annette let the happy sounds wash over her. Too quickly the booted feet stamped on the wooden floor and disappeared outside.

She barely had time to call, "Molly!"

The girl paused at the threshold, one hand on the door. "Yes, Miss Courtney?"

Annette recognized Molly's impatience to be gone

with her friends. Besides, what could she ask for from the little girl? To ask for a hug like a mother receives? An embrace that was demanded held no meaning.

"Be careful going home," she said.

"I will," Molly promised as she dashed through the door.

No one else remained in the schoolroom.

Slowly Annette made her way between the rows. She realigned the benches knocked askew in the hasty departure, stacked the slates neatly on a table, and banked the fire in the new stove. It did a much better job of warming than the old one, but there was no need to heat an empty room. With the students gone, she was more aware of the size of the warehouse. Its hollowness pressed down on her. She poked angrily at the fire before slamming the stove door shut. Somehow her dream of a village school did not satisfy her. She felt as hollow and empty as the warehouse.

After all, the children were not really hers. She could no longer fool herself with the pretense that they were.

Chapter Nine

The clerk showed Annette into the solicitor's office. Mr. Keller came from around his desk to greet her and offer her a chair. The room felt as closed in and stuffy as the last time she had visited.

When she had been seated and the pleasantries dealt with, Annette asked, "You wanted to see me?"

"Yes." Mr. Keller had returned to his desk and now busied himself with a stack of papers there. "I need to discuss with you some improvements the mill steward is recommending for his shop. He would like to bring in some new machinery."

"Surely if he recommends it, I would agree with him. He is the one most knowledgeable about the matter, after all."

"True, true." He handed her the steward's letter.

Annette read it slowly and carefully. The facts seemed to support the steward's request. She did not fully understand everything about this new machinery, but her impression was it would make the work faster, safer, and more productive. She did not know enough to question his assertions.

She handed the letter back to the solicitor. "I do not know enough to question his request. If you think it best, I agree with the purchase."

Mr. Keller steepled his hands. "This new machinery is probably well worth the expense, but you want to be careful that you do not agree to every request. That way lies to waste."

Her lips tightened at the admonishment. Waste was something never associated with her actions. "I am more familiar with my school than a mill."

"Yes." Mr. Keller wrote approved on the steward's letter before setting it aside. Then he turned his attention back to her. "How is your school doing?"

"The children are learning their alphabet and numbers. Some of them are already reading. I am very pleased with the results." She emphasized the last.

Mr. Keller pulled another sheet of paper from his stack. "The costs so far have not been unreasonable. The warehouse renovation was not as expensive as I had feared, and you obtained a good price on the stove."

His condescending attitude caused Annette to tighten her grip in her lap. "I had believed I could spend *my* money as I wished."

"Of course, of course." Mr. Keller wagged a playful finger at her. "But I would be remiss in my duties as a trustee if I did not oversee the expenses."

"The other trustees are satisfied. Indeed, the Reverend Browne is very pleased with the progress the children are making in their reading. He wants them to know their Bible."

"And the baronet?"

"He will probably help the successful students find a situation. The school's results are intangible, not to be found in the balancing of pence." Annette hoped he would not question her more closely about the baronet's involvement. Sir Gerard had never said anything about finding positions for the boys.

"If that's how you wish to spend your money." Mr. Keller let the disapproving statement trail off, as he pulled a sheaf of papers from one of the piles on his desk. He handed them to her.

"What are these?" she asked.

"They are letters of appeal from a variety of charitable societies. Sir Nigel had no interest in such things, so I always threw the appeals out. Since you are interested in intangible results, I thought I should pass them along to you." The solicitor settled back in his chair with a satisfied smile.

Annette smoothed the papers. "I will review these and let you know my decision about them." She glanced through them briefly. "Obviously I handle the fortune differently than Sir Nigel expected, so I am still puzzled as to why he left it to me."

"Why question it? Isn't it enough that you are the heiress?"

She shook her head. "No, for I am starting to wonder if it was spite that is the cause of my good fortune."

"Hmmm." Mr. Keller tapped his fingers together. "You are aware that the former baronet hated his heir." At her nod, he continued, "Sir Nigel never intended to let Sir Gerard get his hands on the money. He intended to leave him as penniless as possible. If not you, then someone else would be the recipient. You were always around, meddling, so he chose you."

"So it was spite."

"The reason does not matter. Look forward to all the good you plan to do, not backwards."

"The reason provides the foundation to the future." Her voice was so quiet, it was almost a whisper. "I wonder if I can do good when it is an injustice that made it possible."

A frown wrinkled the man's face. "What better result to an injustice than that good should result from it?"

"Perhaps, but I do understand Sir Gerard's frustration." She stood to take her leave. "I am not sure if I like being a part of such an injustice."

The solicitor patted her shoulder in a fatherly fashion. "Do not let it trouble you. It would bother no one else."

Later that evening, Annette and Lucille stitched garments to be distributed to the indigent babies of the village. Each woman bent close to the light of their shared lamp. Even though Annette kept the fire built up in the drawing room, she continued to practice frugality.

Tonight she wore a sensible dark blue gown. It still took some adjusting to the idea that a dress could be pretty and practical. Lucille had dressed in a new green one trimmed with a braid in a darker shade. An elegant shawl draped around her shoulders. No longer did it need to be clutched close for warmth.

The fire popped merrily from the sap in the wood. The smell of burning pine lightly scented the air.

"You did not tell me much about your drive with Mr. Linton yesterday," Lucille remarked.

"There was nothing to tell."

"He appears to be a very personable man."

Annette concentrated on placing her stitches in an even row along the sleeve seam. "I want more than a personable man in a marriage."

"Marriage!" Lucille dropped her work in her lap as she stared at her friend. "Do you mean he proposed to you?"

Annette bit her tongue—a few words too late. She had never meant to reveal Linton's offer. "Every single man proposes to me," she said bitterly. "But what they really want is control of my fortune."

"Every one?" Fascinated, Lucille questioned further. "How many offers have you received?"

"I have not kept count."

"I would have." The other woman picked the baby gown. "Why did you refuse Mr. Linton? I liked him well enough."

"He is nice enough for a party or a carriage drive," Annette conceded. "He appears shallow to me. Nothing interests him except for the London social round."

"It does sound like fun."

"Not as a way of life." Annette's firm tone contrasted sharply with the other woman's wistfulness.

The room grew quiet as the women returned to their sewing. Annette used the task in an attempt to banish her disappointment at Linton's offer. She wished the man existed who saw her and not the fortune when he proposed. Yesterday afternoon's echoing schoolroom showed how empty she was without a family of her own. Other people's children were not a substitute for a mate.

"If an ease in society is not what you want in a husband, then what are you looking for?"

Annette sighed. Plainly, once Lucille got a notion in her head, she would pursue it until satisfied. "I do not know . . . I never actually drew up a list."

From the expression on Lucille's face, she expected to have a catalog of attributes recited on the spot. Annette continued, "He should be more than some ornament of the *haute ton*. He should care about the plight of others and do something to help them."

Lucille sniffed. "You want a serious-minded reformer just like yourself."

Stung, Annette responded, "And what is wrong with that?"

"Such a man would be exactly the wrong type of husband for you. You don't need more noble sobriety in your life. You need gaiety or else you will grow into a very unhappy, severe woman."

Her words hurt, and Annette lashed back. "Gaiety? You think that should be my primary goal? It sounds like you would recommend Sir Gerard to be my husband."

Lucille's eyes widened. "Has he asked you yet?"

"Of course not. Unlike you, he knows I would never entertain such a notion."

"Hmmm." Pursing her lips, the other woman bent over her sewing.

Annette continued, "He would be an impossible choice. A man with no sense of responsibility towards others." A twinge of shame pricked her conscience at this proclamation.

It was not completely true.

"Does he make you laugh?"

The question momentarily threw Annette off balance. "Sometimes," she admitted. "Yet that is not enough for me."

"Laughter smoothes many a bump in a marriage," Lucille observed from her status as a widow.

"Yes, but I believe likemindedness reduces the number of bumps."

Her friend did not disagree. "The baronet would be a good catch for you."

For a silent moment, Annette finished stitching the sleeve into the garment. She cut the thread and threw the baby gown down on her lap. "I do not want him to think solely of the money," she burst out. "I want to be important to him, too."

"The money is hard to overlook," Lucille replied softly.

A small smile creased Annette's face. "I know. I find I cannot even overlook it myself." She leaned towards her friend. "Sometimes, I even wish I had not inherited that fortune."

Lucille stared. "But you are doing so much good with it! Why you have even started the school you dreamt of for so long!"

"Yes." Annette gazed into the flames flickering on the hearth. The fire warmed her on the outside, but within she remained hollow and cold. Not even to her closest friend would she reveal how little the students satisfied her need for a family of her own. Was it because an old man's spite had given her the opportunity?

Shaking off her pensive mood, she said brightly, "Jack is doing very well."

"Jack?"

"You know him. He is the oldest son of Tim Farmer who has the tenancy of Springwood farm."

When Lucille nodded, Annette continued, "Jack learned his entire alphabet within one morning's lesson. Already he is reading simple sentences, and he tries to make his writing very neat. Sooner than I anticipated, I will need to speak with Sir Gerard about finding a position for the boy."

"Perhaps you should not wait."

"What do you mean?"

"It might be wiser to alert the baronet of your plans.

Then he can begin to look around for a likely post that can be filled immediately."

Annette glanced sharply at the other woman, but her face was bent diligently over her sewing. She appeared a pattern card of industrious womanhood. Lucille was a woman without guile, and her momentary suspicions shamed Annette. Her friend would never be guilty of such blatant matchmaking attempts. "You are right. I should bring Jack to Sir Gerard's attention. It could be the boy's great chance in life."

"When will you go?"

"Tomorrow, after school lets out. It will not be too late to pay a call."

"You should not wait," Lucille assured her.

While she waited for the butler to announce her call to Sir Gerard, Annette wondered again if she was being hood-winked by Lucille. Jack was just a beginner with his reading and writing. It might be a bit too soon to be looking for a clerkship on his behalf. Indeed, she had not even broached the possibility to him. Maybe the boy would not be interested.

Nonsense. She nodded firmly to herself. A clerkship would be his chance to better himself. Although his father, a good man, worked as a tenant farmer, Jack could do better for himself.

"Sir Gerard will receive you now," the butler said.

She followed him down the hall with its gleaming black and white marble tiles. The tables and chairs shone from the vigorous polishing of beeswax they now received. The clean smell signaled the refurbishing of the hall. The damp, which had been the regular state of the house during winter, was banished by a buildup of fires in

various rooms. The heat provided even seeped into the
front entrance, where it warmed her face. Under the new
master, Hathaway Hall gleamed. She could not help noticing how Sir Gerard honored his responsibilities. Hope for
Jack's chances stirred within her.

In the drawing room, Sir Gerard stood at her entrance.
"Good afternoon, Miss Courtney." To Newton, he placed
a request for tea.

She returned his greeting and observed how he carefully placed her chair just the right distance from the fire.
He did not seat himself until she was comfortable. Waiting for the tea to arrive, they conversed about his London
life and some of her lighter village interests. He made her
feel welcome in the way he paid attention to her remarks
and responded to them. A far different effect than the one
his uncle engendered within her whenever she called upon
Sir Nigel. Inside, she felt her stiffness and wariness soften.

Once the tea had been poured and she had nibbled at
her cake, Annette cleared her throat as she prepared to do
battle on Jack's behalf.

"Is that the signal for the charge?" Sir Gerard asked.

At a loss, she stared at him. "What do you mean?"

"As much as I would like to pretend otherwise, I believe you have a habit of calling upon the current baronet
with a list of demands."

She nearly choked on the crumbs of her cake. "I never
make demands, sir. Only requests."

"What are your *requests* for this call?"

His eyes twinkled, and she realized he was teasing her
again. Once more she had misread him. It made her fear
that Lucille's assessment of her severe attitude might be
correct.

She attempted to respond in a lighter tone. "I have only one request this time."

"Ah." Leaning back in his brocaded wing chair, Sir Gerard sipped his tea. "I almost fear one request more than a list. A single one may be more than I can handle."

Not for a moment did she believe this protestation. "One of my students is doing extremely well with his learning. Although he is the son of one of your tenants, I think a clerk apprenticeship would be appropriate for him. You could find such a position for him." Her speech was not the smooth presentation she had intended, but at least she managed to state everything.

He lifted an eyebrow. "How long has your school been opened?"

"Almost a month." She realized where his question was aiming. "I know it has only been opened a short time, but because he has learned so quickly, I am here on his behalf."

"Does he expect me to find him such a position?"

"No, I have not yet broached the matter to him."

With a troubled frown on his face, Sir Gerard set down his teacup. "I am glad of that. I would not want you to raise impossible hopes."

She feared the meaning behind those words. "Sir, Jack is an excellent student."

"I have no doubt of that. But, Miss Courtney, he is the son of a tenant farmer. Is it right to take him out of his class?"

Her lips tightened. "If he possesses the ability to do so, yes. God expects each of us to use the capabilities He has bestowed upon us."

Sir Gerard held up a hand as if to stop the flow of her words. "Do not repeat to me the parable of the men with talents. I already have heard it. I am more accustomed to a society where everyone knows his place. I know where I belong."

"The times are changing," she said in a softer tone. "We are discovering how important it is to use the talents of everyone, whether an aristocrat or a tenant farmer."

"Yes, I know the reformers are right in the end." He smiled ruefully. "But I liked it better when I knew I was destined for the top of the heap. Now you are changing the foundation beneath me."

"Not just me." Looking at him, she saw the elegance of his life in the tailored manner in which his jacket fit his shoulders and narrowed at the waist. His waistcoat was of a fine embroidered broadcloth. Buckskin stretched over his well-shaped legs. Yet during their drive, Mr. Linton had revealed what it had taken the baronet to achieve his position in society. In his own way, Sir Gerard had been using his God-given talents. "Besides, it has always been the duty of gentry to look out for the interests of those under their care."

"*Touché*, Miss Courtney." He rubbed a hand under his smoothly shaven chin. "You truly think he is ready for a clerk position now?"

She hesitated. Honesty forced her to tell the truth. "Perhaps not exactly at this moment, but very soon. Jack is a very bright boy. It will not take him much longer to learn his skills."

"So you said." He drummed his fingers on the arm of the chair.

Holding her breath, Annette watched him closely. This moment he would decide, and she did not want her slightest movement to tip the decision against her.

"It still seems too soon to me, but—" He shook his

head to forestall her incipient protest. "I will keep an eye open for a position for a likely lad."

Pleasure at her success poured through her like the warmth of the tea. "Thank you, sir. Jack deserves this opportunity."

His gaze studied her, and she met it directly. She had never been shy when requesting help for others. Indeed, many times it was her refusal to be cowed by a loud lecture on the dissolute habits of the poor that gained her the coins she needed.

Yet this time no lecture from the baronet greeted her request. Unlike his uncle, Sir Gerard served a full-bodied tea with an overflowing dish of cakes. She could even eat two of them without a noticeable difference in the pile. Now his eyes gazed steadily into hers. In their dark depths she read liking and a hint of gentle amusement. A slight smile curved his lips, as if he knew how this call had not followed the path set by his uncle. He was a man who set his own path. Unaccountably, she felt a blush steal onto her cheek.

She took refuge in sipping her tea and then set the cup down on the table with a clatter. Perhaps it was too much hot tea that made her feel so overheated and awkward.

Taking herself in hand, Annette continued, "While we are on the subject of your tenants, I would like to bring up the conditions of some of their cottages. They are in horrible shape."

Sir Gerard leaned back in his chair, the smile still on his face. "Fie on you, Miss Courtney! Despite all your admonitions to me, you appear to possess gambling tendencies yourself."

"Gambling? Me? Never!"

"Oh, indeed, yes." His grin stretched wide with wicked

teasing. "Since you are pushing your run of luck with me, you are acting like any lucky bettor who does not know when to leave the table."

The flush on her face burned hotter. "Are you not concerned about the tenants' cottages?"

The amusement fled from his face. "Of course I am, but there is nothing I can do at this moment. There are a thousand demands upon this estate, and I can satisfy none of them."

"Because of your gambling tendencies?" she asked quietly.

"No! Because the money that should have been used for these needs no longer belongs to the estate."

She dropped her gaze to the floor. "I do regret that. You know it was not my doing."

Leaning forward, he took her hand in his. His touch was gentle as his fingers curled around her palm. Strength lay in his grip. Calluses showed the work he had done with the horses.

"I know that now." His thumb rubbed over the back of her hand. "I can turn this estate around. It will take time, but there is a sound basis allowing it to produce the necessary rents. Someday I will be able to take care of the tenants."

"But they suffer so now!"

She could feel the heat of his grasp through her gloves. Even if it were highly improper, she made no move to withdraw her fingers. The kid fabric stretched over her hand like a second skin, offering no barrier to her awareness of his touch.

"You are quite a fierce champion for others." Sir Gerard's voice was soft, but she heard the sincere admiration underlying his words.

Rattled, she assumed a brusque attitude. "I believe it is my Christian duty to help those less fortunate."

"Is it only duty that drives you so strongly?"

"What else could there be?"

"A stronger emotion perhaps," he said. "One such as hate."

Annette jerked herself upright bumping the table, but he did not release her hand. Some of her tea slopped over the cup's edge, but she ignored it. "I do not hate anyone!"

He eyed her intently. "No," he said slowly, "I believe you do not. I think, more than duty, it is love which motivates you."

She gaped at him. "Love?"

"Yes, love. You may call it your duty or Christian charity or any other term, but actually your heart is so big and so full that it encompasses everyone you meet."

Annette blinked. "You are being foolish, sir. I never thought of such a thing."

"Of course not. You are always so busy thinking of others that you never look at yourself. Tell me, Miss Courtney, what was your opinion of my uncle?"

She hesitated. "Why, only that he was so tight with his money I had to show him where his duty as baronet lay."

Nodding, Sir Gerard exclaimed, "You prove my point. My uncle knew his duty, but since he was a selfish, old man, he refused to do it. Only you could demand it from him."

Annette mulled over his words for a moment. Sir Gerard offered her an entirely different perspective of her life. "I never thought of it that way."

"No, you assume only the good intentions of others."

"I think I prefer believing in the good rather than being

suspicious of everyone I meet. After all, I know these people in Upper Brampton."

He withdrew his hand. "Yes, Upper Brampton is your domain, just as London is mine."

Now that her hand was free, Annette was conscious of the loss of his grip's warmth. The coolness made her feel a little bereft, but for what she did not know. "Perhaps one day I should go to London. Lucille is always urging me to go."

"I wonder what the *haute ton* would make of you."

"Society and I?" Annette giggled. "I would never fit in. No, I would like to go to London to talk with some of the groups which are working so hard to improve the lot of the lower classes."

"Your London is very different than mine." Abruptly, he stood and strode over to the window.

The heavy draperies framing the glass still hung open, despite the approaching dusk. The firelight danced on his form, leaving the walls in shadow. Silhouetted against the window, he looked very alone against the outside murkiness. Annette's heart stirred within her.

Rising, she went to his side. When he turned to look at her, she said, "If I went, would you show me your London?"

His hand cupped her chin. "You are a good woman, Miss Courtney. Probably too good for my London. But, yes, I would show my city to you."

Still holding her, he bent forward. His lips lightly brushed hers. At his soft touch, she felt his tentative question and stayed still in response.

She did not pull away, and he remained to kiss her longer and more fully. Annette's first surprise was how sweet his touch tasted. Her second was how tender he was.

Since her inheritance, she had been kissed. Those had been eager, wet things she had no interest in repeating. This one was different. A little uncertain, she found herself matching it move for move, reveling in the exploration.

His arms embraced her as her own hands experimentally crept up his chest. Beneath the rough tweed of his jacket, she could feel the strong breadth of his shoulders.

This man continually bewildered her. He never was who she had expected. Thinking to meet a wastrel, she found a man with the well-exercised body of a horse trainer. Expecting a miser, she encountered a man as concerned about Hathaway Hall's tenants as she was. But when she disbelieved his reputation as a gambler, she paid off a money-lender.

At this reminder, she stiffened in his arms. His embrace loosened, but he did not release her.

"What is it?" he asked.

"This is most inappropriate behavior," she told him in her primmest manner.

Smiling, he stroked her hair. "I know. Didn't you enjoy it?"

"I never enjoy inappropriate behavior."

"Then, since you liked it, the behavior must not be inappropriate."

She blinked at him. So easily and so quickly he could confound her. The effect of his charm and his nearness rattled her. To avoid responding to his quip, she pushed herself free from him. He released her immediately, but the smile did not vanish from his lips nor did the laughter disappear from his eyes.

To escape his gaze, she looked outside the window. "Goodness! I had not realized how late it was. I had best be returning home."

"I will have your carriage summoned." Once the butler had been instructed, Sir Gerard turned back to her, the gentle amusement still existent upon his face. "I look forward to the next time you call with a request on someone else's behalf."

From the twinkle in his eye, she knew he remembered their kiss. Did he think every request would end with one? She tried to respond resolutely, but something within her giggled at his teasing. "It should not take me long to find another need."

Momentarily, the teasing cleared from his demeanor. "Unfortunately, I know I can rely on that. The distress of these people is so great."

As she headed back home in her carriage, Annette pondered their meeting. Sir Gerard was so mercurial she could not easily slot him under a label. A gambler certainly, yet not a miser. He obviously loved to tease. Witness that sally about love not duty being her inspiration. Yet, when the subject of his tenants' poverty arose, so did his concern. She highly approved of those sentiments.

Did she also approve of the kiss? Annette gently ran her fingers over her lips, trying to re-create his touch. She only felt kid gloves brushing her mouth. Only he could duplicate that touch. Although she did not want to admit it, she had enjoyed the kiss, despite its obvious inappropriateness.

Firmly placing her hand on her lap, she shook herself free from these musings. Sir Gerard had made his way through the world using his charm. Naturally a kiss would be a part of his arsenal. How could she rely on such a man? No matter how much he intrigued her, no matter how much she liked him, no matter how much she wanted to meet him again, she must remember to keep her guard up.

Still, as the carriage jounced through the evening light, Annette wished she knew if the kiss meant something or was it only a homage to the moneybags?

Chapter Ten

The alarm arrived at Hathaway Hall several hours after midnight. By the light of the flickering candle held by his valet, Sir Gerard blinked the sleep from his eyes as he sought to comprehend what his valet was saying.

"A fire?" Sir Gerard repeated the message groggily.

"Yes, sir. One of the tenant farms. It is blazing even now."

The baronet pushed aside the bedcovers, flinching as the cold night air hit his sleep-warmed body. "My clothes. I must dress immediately. Send for Silver Shadow to be ready to ride."

The valet scurried to obey, asking, "Sir, do you intend to ride there in the middle of the night?"

"I do. Which tenant is it?"

"Tim Farmer."

Sir Gerard strode to the window and looked out. A cloud covered the half-moon, providing little light, but there was enough snow on the ground to reflect the small amount of illumination. "His farm lies between here and the village, correct?"

"Yes, sir." The valet had laid out his master's clothing.

Sir Gerard began to dress. "Who brought the news?"

"I am not sure, sir. It may have been one of the neighbors."

It did not really matter who actually brought the alert. The important duty was to respond to it. He dressed quickly, forgoing a cravat in place of a woolen muffler.

Within minutes, he rode through the Wiltshire night. The cold air stung, but fortunately there was no wind. The fire could be contained if stray sparks were doused as quickly as they landed. He hoped the farm owned a good producing well. During his early morning rides, he had ridden past the farm, but other than its location, he could not remember much about it.

Although he wanted to send Silver Shadow through the night at top speed, the erratic light made such a course dangerous. Snow caused the path to be slippery, even as it boosted the moonlight. Barren branches etched dark lines into the night, deepening the shadows beneath them.

Only the sound of his horse's hooves cracking through the thin layer of ice covering the mud broke the night's silence. The animals must all be shivering in their burrows. Not even the screech of a successful hunting owl sounded.

Sir Gerard smelled the fire before he reached it. At first, it scented the air with wood smoke. Yet all too soon, the light smell gave way to the thick fumes warning of the disaster ahead.

Silver Shadow shied beneath his rider. Gently but firmly, Sir Gerard calmed his mount and urged him forward.

The scene at the farmhouse resembled the hellish disaster it was. The fire had passed the stage where an organized effort might have saved something. The heavy smoke clogged the air, causing his eyes to water. The strength of the blazing inferno had melted the snow in the trampled yard into a muddy morass. Only the roar of its consuming appetite resounded in the farmyard.

Hastily roused neighbors clustered in despairing silence, watching the destruction of the cottage. Buckets and rags to prevent the fire from spreading hung from their hands, but the cottage was lost. Already the roof and walls were ablaze with the orange glow.

At Sir Gerard's approach, their sullen stares swiveled towards him. No one moved to hold his horse as he dismounted. Holding the reins in his hand, he strode forward. With all of their eyes focused upon him, he felt like he walked into a wall far more substantial than the smoke hovering over the yard.

This passive distrust was a part of his uncle's legacy. For too long, Sir Nigel had snatched the fruits of their labor and never returned a farthing he was not forced to. Now, when one of their own faced destitution, they did not expect help from the baronet.

Sir Gerard squared his shoulders. He was not his uncle. "Which one of you is Tim Farmer?"

A stout man with a soot-streaked face and begrimed clothing pushed himself forward. "That's me."

Conscious of the other listening ears, Sir Gerard said, "I am sorry to see this destruction. How did it happen?"

The other man took a deep breath and straightened to his full height. "It were the chimney. It's been bad for years, but no repairs ever got done on it. Fire started in it. Could have smoldered for hours and us never know it. It always gave off smoke." With a final condemnation, he added, "And no repairs done even though I asked."

A low growl from the crowd emphasized the truth of the man's words. They probably had similar stories. Sir

Gerard could feel their hostility, as if the fire had burned away the restraints of civilization even as it consumed the home. Danger threatened. Perhaps he should not have come, but this man was one of his tenants.

"That neglect was shameful. It will not happen again."

Tim eyed him truculently. "Fine words from a baronet."

"I mean them," Sir Gerard said. "Is your family safe?"

"Me wife and son got out. We're not hurt." Tim's fists were clenched, but he made no threatening move.

"I am glad they escaped." Sir Gerard's lips thinned as he looked at the destruction. "I will make sure your home is rebuilt."

"Aye, and raise my rents to boot, I'll be bound."

"No, I mean to make up for the hardship you have suffered in the past. Your cottage will be rebuilt, and the chimney will be safe this time."

Disbelief and hope warred across the farmer's blunt face. "But what am I going to do now? How will I care for my family? It is winter."

The urge to help this man rushed through Sir Gerard. Against the backdrop of crackling flames, he wanted to encourage Tim's hope. He gazed beyond the crowd, seeking a solution. "The barn looks like it is still standing. Could you live in it until the new cottage is built?"

"The barn is all I got left."

"It would work. For a little while." Sir Gerard pushed through the crowd. With an uncertain hesitation, the people parted before him. "It would be a place to start."

Tim came, too, and his glance swept over the building. "But it is winter. How would me wife and son stay warm? I ain't risking another fire."

The enthusiasm for providing this help flared higher

within Sir Gerard even as the roar of the blaze behind him began to subside. He would not let such a small objection about the lack of a chimney prevent him from assisting one of his people in need.

Still pulling Silver Shadow, he strode towards the barn. Tim followed, and behind him the crowd trailed, eavesdropping on everything.

Muttering to himself, Sir Gerard studied the barn, seeking an answer to the problem. The weather-beaten barn sagged from old age like most of the buildings belonging to Hathaway Hall's lands, excepting only the baronet's own house. The flickering light displayed the splintering boards and the cracks in the wall. The cold wind could still whistle its way in. Such a structure might shelter the oxen as a windbreak, but people needed more than a pile of straw to stay warm.

Looking at it, he was reminded of Miss Courtney and her school constructed from a dilapidated warehouse. Were all the buildings of the area on the verge of falling down? He wished he had some of her ability to build something from nothing available now.

Then he was reminded of something else about her school. A broad grin spread across his face. "I've got the answer. You need a stove."

"A stove, sir?" Tim's puzzled look reflected the murmuring of the crowd.

Sir Gerard clapped the man heartily on the back. "It is the perfect solution. I will buy you a stove that will keep your family warm while you are living in the barn. Once your cottage is rebuilt, we can move it into your new home."

Hope sprang alive on the man's ruddy face. "Do you

mean it, sir? You're not just speaking words to me, are you?"

"I mean it," Sir Gerard promised. No matter what he had to do, he was not going to disappoint this man, even if it required building the cottage with his own two hands.

Grabbing his benefactor's hand, Tim shook it as if he were priming a pump. "I'm your man, sir. For all the rest of me days. You don't know what this means to me."

It took some effort, but Sir Gerard managed to free his hand. "Perhaps I do," he said softly, but Tim did not hear him.

He was too busy proclaiming the goodness of Baronet Westcourt. Now the other men pushed forward, wanting to shake Sir Gerard's hand.

The attention embarrassed him, but there was no escape from the now friendly crowd. Several of them attempted to speak of their own problems.

"Not now," Sir Gerard said to those. "It has been a busy night, and everyone needs some rest. I want to help Tim here first. Bring your concerns to me later at Hathaway Hall."

A sudden crash diverted attention back to the fire. One of the cottage walls had fallen in, sending red sparks flying into the night. Some of them landed on the barn, but ready workers slapped the emerging flames into oblivion with their wet rags.

Sir Gerard stepped back while they worked, glad that they managed to save the barn. Already tonight he had promised more than he could pay for. He needed a stove immediately, a cottage quickly, and his own debts were due at the end of the month. This was already late February. He would not have the quarterly funds available until the end of March, and even that amount would not cover all that he now owed. Yet, Tim Farmer and his family could not live in a barn without that stove for the six weeks or more of winter remaining.

Distracted, he ran his hand through his hair. Silver Shadow nudged him, and he spoke quietly to his horse, "What am I going to do, old boy? These people are counting on me. I want to help them. I promised it, but how am I going to keep that promise?"

The horse nickered as if he understood the concern lacing his master's voice.

"You saw how he depends upon my position for relief. How they all do. If only I could get that money." He gave a bitter laugh. "Who am I kidding? Even if I had the quarter funds, it would not be enough to cover my word."

Patting the horse's neck, he continued, "You do not have a very honorable owner. It is a good thing you are only a horse and don't know any better."

As if to belie his words, Silver Shadow nudged him with such strength that Sir Gerard nearly lost his balance.

"Hey!" he cried. "I apologize. I did not mean to offend you. Guess you know a bit more than I realized."

Silver Shadow shook his mane and stamped his hoof.

Sir Gerard chuckled. "I'm glad I'm forgiven." Then he grew serious again. "I am in deep trouble this time. I need the money, and I certainly will not go to that money-lender again."

The horse's snort announced his agreement with his master's opinion.

"If not money-lenders, where else can a man obtain money? Who has some?"

Rubbing his hand along Silver Shadow's nose, Sir Gerard watched the fire. The immediate threat from the sparks had been thwarted, and now the flames finished consuming their prize. The crowd also gazed at the destruction of the cottage, but there was an easing of the tension, as if they, too, realized the immediate battle was over.

Yes, their fight was finished, but Sir Gerard knew his war still continued. The people relied on him to provide, and he did not have any solutions.

Silver Shadow's breath warmed his fingers, returning feeling to Sir Gerard's cold, numbed hand. He mulled over the people who had wealth. They acquired it through lands and other business interests. He had title and land, but still no ready cash. Only money-lenders and bankers had that.

"Bankers," he breathed in sudden realization. "Banks have the money. I can go to a bank for the money I need. I no longer must deal with money-lenders. I am respectable enough for a mortgage—after all I own property."

In his happiness, he hugged his horse with so much enthusiasm that Silver Shadow neighed nervously. Sir Gerard just laughed. He had found his solution. He would place a mortgage on his land. He could pay it off from the quarter rents. No longer would he have debts hanging over his head like a gallow's noose. Despite the smoke pall lingering over the yard, the dawning of the day appeared very bright to Sir Gerard.

The sound of an approaching carriage turned everyone's attention towards the new arrival. A sturdy chestnut pulled a landau into the farmyard. Annette Courtney held the reins. By her side, a blanket covered a lumpy pile.

Sir Gerard strolled to the carriage and bowed. "Good morning, Miss Courtney. You are certainly out early this morning."

Her frank gaze swept over him in astonishment. "Sir Gerard! I am surprised to see you here."

He helped her down from her seat, feeling the curve of her waist as his hands went around her. "When one of my tenants is in trouble, certainly you would expect me to help?"

Stepping back from him, she straightened her gloves. "I may expect such duties from a baronet, but I have not experienced them in the past."

He smiled at her. "I told you before, I am not my uncle."

"So you have said. I am very glad you are not." She cast a glance up at him, and he spotted the humor glinting in her eyes.

He realized she flirted with him like any London lady, and it amazed him. An answering merriment arose within him. He wanted to stay beside her, to continue the art of coquetry that sparked between them. "We covered why I am here, but what brings you out so early?"

"I brought some supplies to assist the Farmer family." She gestured towards the lumpy blanket pile. "I have some jellies and a dressed chicken for them. Of course, they are going to need these blankets, too."

Admiration rushed through him. "Very practical. They do need food and blankets to get through these next few days. But how did you manage to get a chicken ready so quickly?"

"Good housekeeping. A smart woman uses the winter cold to keep her meat from spoiling."

"You mean the chicken was to be your dinner today?"

She shrugged. "Lucille and I really do not eat a whole chicken in one meal."

More and more he recognized what a jewel this woman was. "Then I must insist that both of you join me tonight for dinner."

She raised her eyebrows in surprise. "That is not necessary."

"Yes, it is. I am trying to watch out for the people who depend upon me, which includes Upper Brampton village. You reside there, thus placing you under my care. Will you let me make certain you do not go hungry?"

At her blush, he savored the raillery between them even more. He stepped closer.

She took an unsteady breath and turned to toss the blanket aside, revealing the basket filled with jars and the towel-wrapped chicken. Several tightly rolled blankets surrounded the basket to keep it steady on the seat. A light wisp of steam wavered from the crock of hot soup. It smelled like a good thick chicken broth, confirming to Sir Gerard that Annette would never water down a gift of food.

"Tim Farmer," she called. "I have brought these items for you and your family."

Sir Gerard knew she was avoiding a response to his dinner offer, but he did not press the issue. Instead, he stood silently by the landau, watching as she distributed her goods to the distressed family. The man's profuse thanks and his wife's gratitude could have been overwhelming, but Annette responded graciously.

Her capable hands distributed the largesse. In addition to the supplies on the seat, she had stored items on the floor. These proved to be more foodstuffs, along with dishes and cooking utensils. Neighbors helped to unload everything, but Sir Gerard could not help wondering if Annette had stacked everything in the carriage by herself. Once he had said she did everything for these people; now he saw her generosity in action.

He watched as she spoke with Tim Farmer. "These

items should tide you over for a few days. I will be back
by then with more." She glanced at the smoldering cottage. "Do you know what you are going to do?"

A bright grin carved Tim's stern features. "We're going
to live in the barn."

"The barn?" She assessed it with a quick glance. "Yes,
I can see that is the only solution for now, but you will
need many more blankets to keep warm."

"The baronet, he has it all worked out," Tim informed
her.

"He does?"

"We are going to live in the barn with a stove, but only
for a bit. Then he is going to build me a new cottage—
with a working chimney this time."

She glanced over at Sir Gerard, the disbelieving question plain on her face.

Sir Gerard answered, "Yes, I will do all that."

She blinked as if in disbelief, but her smile was filled
with approval. "You will? How good of you! How very
good of you."

Sir Gerard heard the lilting note of approval in her
voice. Like music, it struck a responding chord within
him. He liked gaining her regard and wanted to linger in
it longer. "Come with me. Please."

Grasping her hand, he tugged her away from the landau
and the crowd. She went with him willingly. When they
were a little ways apart from everyone else, he stopped.
Silver Shadow's reins remained looped around his master's arm.

"What is it?" she asked.

He faced her, suddenly at a loss for words. She stood
very straight in her serviceable wool coat with a practical
bonnet tied firmly on her head. Wisps of hair strayed loose

underneath it after her early morning ride. A dark-colored dress peeked beneath the hem of her coat. Heavy leather gloves protected her hands when driving. He had seen those same capable hands at work relieving the misery of others. Annette Courtney was not a society woman, but her spirit shone through her plain trappings like a white light. Probably no one else recognized it.

But he did.

And it drew him to her like an enchantment. He wanted to tarry near her. Almost without realizing it, he said, "Annette, I want to marry you."

Her jaw dropped open. "What?"

"I want to marry you," he repeated, knowing even as he spoke that it was the truth.

She was not the type of woman he had ever planned to wed, yet he now knew how small-minded his list of wifely attributes had been. This was the woman he wanted. Her heart was so big, so full of love for all, that he wanted to share in it for the rest of his life.

"Why on earth would you want to marry me?"

Even as he fumbled for the words to express his deep admiration, the bewilderment in her eyes hardened to anger.

Annette wrenched her hand free from his grasp. "I understand now, sir! And it is a despicable plan! Unworthy of you."

He stared at her. "What plan?"

"To use these people's tragedy in such a manner. I understand your scheme," she declared. "First you make promises of help you are unable to finance, and then you expect to gain control of the fortune through marriage to me. You thought to use my concern for your tenants to force my agreement to your proposal."

"Force? I had no intention of forcing you to agree." The accusation stung more acutely because he had not even considered the money when he proposed. His misreading of her clear generosity had lured him to speak rashly. "It was an honest proposal made to a woman I thought I admired."

"Admired?" There was a wealth of disbelief in her voice.

"Yes, admired," he said bitterly. "Although at present I could not state why. The money has so twisted your perspective that you see everything through it."

She paled. "No, I do not want to believe that."

"Then how else do you explain how my proposal leads you to immediately suspect a sly trick?"

He spun around to remount Silver Shadow, but she reached out a hand to stay him.

"What can I suppose except a trick? You are not the first man to recently offer for me. I am well aware which of my features attracts them, and it is a fiscal one not a physical one. Even at our first meeting, you promised to regain the fortune." Her voice softened. "I believe you meant that."

"I did mean it." Turning away from the horse, he looked at her. "Yet, this morning I forgot about the money. My offer is a sincere one."

She attempted to smile. "Made to a woman you admired?"

"One whom I still do." Realizing his words spoke truly, he took her hand in his.

Her rueful gaze met his squarely. "Please forgive my mistake."

"You well know that I am very familiar with making

mistakes. I appreciate the opportunity to not be the transgressor for a change."

She laughed at his rejoinder.

At her humor, the hurt of her rejection eased. "I still expect to see you and Mrs. Downes at Hathaway Hall tonight for dinner."

"You are very generous, but—"

"I do not want to hear any excuses."

When she opened her mouth in dispute, he leaned towards her. She became motionless, waiting. He silenced her protest with a kiss. She stood still within his embrace, and he felt her lips cool and smooth beneath his. Her touch lured him onwards. Unable to stop himself, he deepened the kiss, trying to understand this woman who attracted him so. What was it about her that fascinated him? Attempts at logic disappeared when she began to return his kiss. He pulled her closer as if his grasp could hold all of her soul and felt her body mold to his.

Silver Shadow's head butted him in the back, staggering his balance and recalling him to his whereabouts. Looking up, but still keeping his arm around Annette, Sir Gerard realized how quiet the farmyard had become. Except for the muted burning roar from the smoldering fire and the stamp of his horse's hooves, no sound broke the silence. The crowd watched them with great interest.

"It seems we have an audience," he told her.

"Oh, no!" She flung her hands before her face in mortified horror. "What have I done?"

"Shall we do it again?" He reached for her, but Annette pushed him away.

"I have never been so humiliated."

"Don't be," he assured her and put one arm around her.

"How can I face them?"

"With confidence. Like this." Turning to the crowd, he swept off his hat and bowed deeply to them. His arm around her shoulders caused her to join his gesture. A scattering of claps and shouts replied. The sounds crescendoed when he bowed to Annette and kissed her hand. Jauntily replacing his hat, he mounted Silver Shadow. "I shall expect to see you tonight with your answer to my proposal."

After a wink at her, he guided his horse away from the farmyard.

Chapter Eleven

Confusion filled Annette as she watched Sir Gerard trot gaily away. Humor, embarrassment, and exasperation whirled within her. Upon which emotion should she fasten? It infuriated her at how that man could mix her up.

Resolutely she turned her gaze away from watching his departure. She would not act like some lovesick fool! Yet when she faced the avidly curious eyes of her neighbors, she knew that was exactly the label they pinned on her.

No one had moved, but approving grins and sly smiles painted their faces. An unwanted flush stole over her. To counteract it, she called out in a dictatorial manner, "I still have some supplies here to be unloaded!"

Her abruptness did not bother the crowd, and they moved to help. If anything, the smirks grew more pronounced, just like the heat she could feel radiating from her face.

"Mrs. Farmer," she said, "you should point out where you want these items set. It would save time rearranging later."

"Thank you, Miss Courtney. I'll do that."

Feeling even more embarrassed at telling such a competent woman her business, Annette tugged at her gloves. "If you want to keep Jack home from school for the next day or so, I will understand. Just do not make his absence extend too long. He is doing very well in his studies."

Surprised, Mrs. Farmer paused in refolding a blanket. "You will be keeping on with the school then?"

"Keep it on? Of course. Why would I close down the school?"

The farmwife cast a significant glance down the road. "It looks to me like you're going to be busy with a husband."

Annette also looked down the lane. "I am not marrying the baronet. And even if I did, the school would remain open."

"When a woman marries, her husband's wishes come first." Mrs. Farmer pursed her lips. "I heard tell the baronet weren't too pleased about your school."

Since that was the truth, Annette could not argue against it. "I am not marrying Sir Gerard."

Mrs. Farmer shrugged. "So you say. But I always figured you to be a woman who didn't spread her kisses around lightly."

Annette could only gape in helpless frustration. She did not kiss every man in sight, but protesting would only further confirm the other's supposition. Drat that man! She wished he was still within earshot so she could tell him what she thought of him. Naturally *he* had made good his escape—after kissing her in front of every man and his wife.

Gathering her skirts in one hand, Annette climbed into her landau. Attempting to regain her dignity, she said in a regal tone, "You may rest assured that the school will remain open. Please be sure to pass that word among the others who may wonder."

"I'll do it." The woman's tone was respectful, but Annette suspected its deference.

"If you need more food or other supplies, let me know. I will see about obtaining them."

"Thank you kindly, Miss Courtney. We shouldn't need too much, since the baronet will so quickly rebuild our home."

There was no mistaking the admiration Mrs. Farmer displayed for Sir Gerard. Annette tightened her lips. She suspected how that project was to be funded. She must take the matter up with the baronet at dinner tonight.

She managed to reply graciously. "I am glad he is taking care of his tenants so well."

"It must be your influence." Mrs. Farmer nodded at the thought. "You're a good woman, and he's a good catch. You've done well for yourself, but it's no more than you deserve."

Annette controlled herself with what she considered to be admirable forbearance. "I think you are a trifle premature."

The woman smirked. "We will see."

"Good day, Mrs. Farmer." Annette slapped the reins across the horse's rump, and the landau wheeled out of the yard.

While she drove home, she had plenty of time to reflect on Sir Gerard and his maddening actions. How dare he kiss her so boldly! He must have known it would mark her as his in everyone's eyes. She most certainly did not want to be his. Did she?

Annette remembered how good it felt to be in his arms. For a moment, everything else had faded away. Not even her concern for those burned out of their home had crossed her mind. Only Sir Gerard had dominated her senses.

When she had accused him of using the fortune to re-build the cottage, his surprise seemed genuine. Now she wondered how he intended to pay for everything. Was she misjudging him?

A tiny bit of optimism burgeoned within her as she admitted to hoping she was wrong. A man with a compassionate nature was one she could care for. Lulled by the steady beat of the horse's hooves against the frozen road, she drifted into a daydream where she married Sir Gerard and together they eased the needy misery in Upper Brampton village and its countryside.

She was picturing the thanks from a family for a new well, when she remembered she had yet to answer Sir Gerard's proposal. She shook herself free from the fantasy so fiercely that she tugged on the reins, causing the horse to slow.

With a cluck and a slap of the reins, she urged the animal forward. This inattention was plain foolishness. She needed to carefully think about Sir Gerard's offer.

The crowd at the farmyard expected her school to close. She would never permit that to happen. And then there was the money-lender. What did his presence indicate about the baronet's character?

When Annette entered her dining room, her inner tumult must have appeared on her face, for Lucille dropped her slice of toast.

"Oh, Annette, what happened out there? Don't tell me someone was hurt."

"No, no one was injured, but the Farmers lost their entire cottage."

"How awful! What are they going to do now?"

Annette seated herself at the table and began to fill her plate. All the morning's excitement had sharpened her hunger. "They are going to live in their barn until Sir Gerard rebuilds their cottage."

"The baronet? What was he doing there?"

Annette told her about his plans.

"That's news well worth smiling about," Lucille said. She eyed her friend carefully, but Annette concentrated on smoothing jelly on her toast. "So why are you so upset?"

"I am not upset."

"Something is certainly bothering you. I should think you would be glad the new baronet is taking such an interest in his tenants. It's what you've always demanded."

With an exasperated sigh, Annette set down her food. "I might as well tell you. You will certainly hear about it from everyone else."

Lucille's eyes rounded with curiosity. "Hear what?"

"Sir Gerard kissed me in front of everyone in the farmyard."

"He did!" Lucille clapped her hands in delight. "How wonderful! Annette, he will make you a wonderful husband."

"I have not said I am going to marry him," Annette reminded her. She *had known* that kiss would put such notions into people's minds. She'd known it.

"But you will. After all, you like him, and he apparently cares about you."

"No mention of love, I see."

"Pooh!" Lucille waved her hand in dismissal. "He is titled and handsome. How could you not love him?"

These qualities attracted Annette just as much as his character did. After all, she was a woman as well as a spinster. She wanted to accept Lucille's statements, but hesitated in believing her friend. "Maybe he is just after control of the fortune."

The other woman frowned as she considered this reminder. "You said he intended to rebuild the burned-down cottage. That shows he's a good man."

Since Annette agreed, she brought up the doubt that Mrs. Farmer had provoked, "But what about his opposition to the school?"

"You surely were not planning to teach once you married. That was only a temporary thing."

"I never meant for the school to be temporary."

"If you are so set upon it," Lucille soothed, "it can be one of your charities as the baronet's wife. You can still oversee its running."

It was the daily interaction with the children that Annette enjoyed so much. "You are assuming a whole marriage on the basis of one kiss," she muttered.

"A very public kiss."

Seeing she would get no support from her companion, Annette abandoned that topic. Pouring a cup of tea, she said, "It bothers me that Sir Gerard promised so much to the Farmers."

"*I* think it's wonderful of him to do so."

"But what if he cannot fulfill his pledges?" Annette tore her toast into pieces. "He will leave them worse off because their hopes will be dashed."

"Why would he not rebuild their home?"

"Since I have known him, Sir Gerard has always informed me about his lack of money."

Lucille offered hopefully. "Maybe he found some."

"Maybe, but he never said where he was going to get the funds." Annette stirred the sugar into her tea. "That money-lender bothers me. I do not know much about money management, but I do know one should avoid the cent-percenters at all costs."

In a more subdued tone, Lucille said, "I'm sure there is a reason."

"Perhaps we can find out tonight. He has invited us to dinner at Hathaway Hall."

At this news, animation returned to Lucille, and she began to plan their wardrobes. Content to listen to her friend's bustling, Annette did not dare tell her of Sir Gerard's proposal. Not until she knew herself what her answer would be.

Sir Gerard rode Silver Shadow for a long, glorious trip through the forest and meadows. Despite the February winter, the early morning light sprinkled trees, bushes, and ground with a fresh sparkle. The snow gleamed among the dark bare branches. He spotted a tardy rabbit hurrying for his den. A hidden songbird thrilled a melody that aptly expressed his own feelings of bliss.

That same positive hunch cloaked him which he sometimes sensed when betting on a sure thing. Pictures of Annette flashed again and again through his mind. His attention lingered over the way her face looked that morning with her hair blown astray and concern deep in her eyes. He flicked the reins and remembered her at the Assembly. He smiled at her awkward attempts to flirt and at the determination she had displayed in preventing him from entering the card room. He could no longer think of her as Miss Courtney. Not when he had tasted her lips and held her close.

He had gambled when he kissed Annette, and it still remained to see if this wager would be a winner. But how could he lose?

He did not fully understand why he had proposed. Logic dictated against her as a choice, but logic had never been his strong suit. A man who lived by his wits must learn to rely on instinct as much as rational thought.

During this ride, he soared on his sensations. He relished the strength of Silver Shadow's muscles moving beneath him, the sting of the cold on his nose, but so refreshingly clear in his lungs, and the crunch of his horse's hooves against the crust of the snow.

It was close to midday before he returned to Hathaway Hall. After informing the butler to prepare for dinner guests that evening and receiving his mail, Sir Gerard strolled into the library.

Sprawled on a chair, Linton looked up from the newspaper he was reading. "So at last you've come home. You certainly do keep country hours out here with such early rising."

Shrugging, Sir Gerard began to open his letters. "Town hours will not work in Upper Brampton."

"Nothing works when the countryside is as dead as a doornail," his friend grumbled.

"I am sorry this visit is not to your liking." Sir Gerard's reply was perfunctory as he scanned his mail. The invitation to dinner at the local vicar's was probably not Linton's idea of a good time, but they would go, since it was something to do. The invoices for horse feed and other supplies he set down to handle later.

The last envelope, a thick and creamy one such as a duke might use, intrigued him. He turned it over, but there was no crest imprinted on the sealing wax. Slitting it open, he pulled out the letter.

The signature said Mortimer Wallace. The letter was a demand reminding Sir Gerard the full amount of his loan was due at the end of February. No extensions would be granted. Missing payment would not be a good idea.

His knees wobbled. Sir Gerard stumbled to a chair and fell into it. How could he meet this outrageous ultimatum? The money he intended to raise through a mortgage was earmarked for the estate's needs. He had nothing left to pay off the full debt to Wallace. He could only rely on the quarterly rents to pay the installments. When he had signed the loan, worrying about full payment had not concerned him. He was supposed to be a rich man!

His blissful morning shattered, he rubbed his temple.

"Bad news?"

"It's from Wallace." Sir Gerard answered. He lifted the letter from his lap and stared at it. Although the letters blurred before his stunned gaze, their wording remained the same.

Linton grimaced. "That is bad news. What does he want?"

"He still demands I pay the full loan amount at the end of the month."

"What are you going to do?"

"There is nothing I can do. He will be paid off in the quarterly amounts we originally agreed to. I will send him a letter reminding him of that."

Linton shook his head. "He won't like it. Nasty things happen to those who displease him."

"What can he do?" Sir Gerard asked reasonably, despite the apprehension that shivered down his spine. "He is in London and I am miles away in Upper Brampton—where nothing ever happens."

His attempt at humor recalled his friend to his grievance. "I am not sure which is worse, the weather or the lack of activity." Linton shook the newspaper.

"If you want to go outside for activity, then join me for a morning ride."

Linton shuddered. "Too cold."

"Then you probably would not enjoy outside in London either," Sir Gerard commented. "Perhaps you will take pleasure in the guests I have invited for dinner."

Peering over the newspaper, the other man asked, "Who?"

"Miss Courtney and her companion Mrs. Downes."

"The spinster and the pig farmer's widow."

A burning anger flashed through Sir Gerard. With two steps, he reached Linton's side and snatched the newspaper from his hands. "That rude remark is uncalled for. You will watch your tongue while the ladies are my guests."

His friend stared in astonishment. "Indeed. I know enough to do the pretty at the dinner table."

"It is your lack of respect towards the lady to whom I have offered which concerns me."

"You proposed to the spinster? Good for you!"

Mastering his anger, Sir Gerard released the newspaper. "I hope she accepts me."

"Don't worry, she will," Linton said. "I won't do anything to wreck your chances." Sir Gerard started to smile at the man's assurances, when Linton continued, "When you get your fortune, you won't have any more problems with that money-lender and can escape from this dreary countryside."

Sir Gerard froze, ready to take the man to task. Then his shoulders slumped. What would be the purpose? At one time, even *he* agreed with Linton's plan. Would no one believe that he had proposed without a thought of the money in mind? Not even Annette.

He glanced at the letter lying where it had fallen on the rug. Life would be much simpler if he controlled the fortune. He may not have considered the money when he offered, but it very much dominated his mind now.

Perhaps because he wanted to hear Annette's answer, the day passed slowly until the dinner hour. He busied himself with a letter to the bank about a mortgage and brushed Silver Shadow's coat until the horse impatiently fidgeted under the attention. Then he wandered aimlessly through Hathaway Hall's grounds. The dead grass poked up through the light layer of snow. The air was quiet and still, as befitted the dead of winter. No bird's song trilled to break the silence. No longer did he see the sparkle in nature.

Now dread filled him. He feared her rejection.

At last, dusk fell and the ladies arrived. The welcoming bustle and the exchange of pleasantries occupied the time before they sat down to eat. Throughout the dinner, he tried to interpret Annette. What message did she send? She wore a blue gown made from a silk surely smuggled from France. Was such a dress a good omen? Or did the darkness of the blue mean to dampen his hopes? It was an extravagant choice for her, but it flowed on her with a smooth motion that made him want to kiss her again. Did she feel the same?

Her face offered no clue. In the flickering candlelight, he could not read the depths of her eyes. When he held her close that morning, the clarity of her gaze and the taste of her lips had lured him on.

Tonight she ate the soup and seemed to like the smoked

ham with pickled onions. He tasted nothing himself. Apprehension killed his taste buds.

She laughed at Linton's jokes and smiled uncertainly at his friend's extravagant compliments. He could have told the man that effusive praise only worried his practical Annette, but worry made his own tongue incapable of coherent speech.

After dinner as they returned to the drawing room, Linton said to him in a low tone, "I'll keep doing the pretty with Miss Courtney. She'll be so dazzled by my stories of London society, she'll accept your offer."

"No, she's not that type," Sir Gerard protested, reaching out to halt him, but his friend had already sauntered ahead.

In the drawing room, he poured Linton a glass of brandy and one for himself. The women seated themselves and took the glasses of ratafia he offered. Conversation centered around the doings of the village.

Sipping his brandy smuggled from France like the silk of her dress, Sir Gerard watched her. A log shifted in the fireplace, momentarily sending up a burst of extra light. Against this scene of domestic tranquility, his dinner lay heavy in his stomach. How could he draw her aside to hear her reply?

"Do you intend to go to London this spring?" Linton asked Annette.

"I had not planned to. My school is doing quite well now that it has a new stove." The smile she flashed at Sir Gerard warmed him like the stove must function for her students.

"I was not thinking of a business-related trip, but one of pleasure," Linton said. "The Season is definitely the time to visit the city."

Annette considered his statement. "I do not know how much pleasure there would be going to a city where I am unknown."

Sir Gerard recognized this as his opening. "An entrée into society is what you need. I would be happy to introduce you." He leaned forward to say more, but Linton interrupted.

"Sir Gerard knows everyone. With him to guide you, London can be very exciting."

"Thank you for your very kind offer." Sir Gerard could see that Annette's interest was only polite.

Linton was not finished. "There is so much to do. Lots of people whom you would want to know. Parties and routs and theater—something is always happening. It's exciting and stimulating." The more he exclaimed, the more flushed his face became. He winked at his friend.

Sir Gerard frowned. Could the man not rein in his tongue long enough so he could speak? The social round did not appeal to Annette. He would lose her if Linton kept on.

Lucille said, "How can you ever choose what to do? There sounds like so much."

From the shine in her eyes, Sir Gerard knew Linton had won one supporter.

"So many people sounds overwhelming," Annette commented.

Fearing more of his friend's assistance, Sir Gerard tried to steer the conversation. "It can be overwhelming at first—"

"But that is part of the city's pleasure," Linton inserted. "The array of choices is splendid, not like here. London is lively."

Sir Gerard noticed her stiffening at this disparagement

of Upper Brampton. He hoped his friend would temper his speech, but Linton plunged ahead.

"The balls are grand affairs with an array of food such as you've never seen. The routs are so crowded that one is not considered a success unless the guests are crushed. You can ride in the park and be seen by all the right people," he told her. "You should come to London for the Season."

A frown creased Annette's head. "I could not leave my school for so long."

"Your school? Of course you could leave it. After all, once you are married, you won't be teaching there anyway."

"I am not married yet," Annette remarked with some asperity. "I have no desire to give up my school." She cast a challenging glance at Sir Gerard.

He could not let her reject his offer. His mind raced as he scrambled to persuade her. "There is no need to give up the school. It is a worthy charity." Suspicion still simmered in her eyes. "Perhaps you could hire a teacher."

She started to protest, then mulled over his idea. "It would not be the same."

"No," he agreed. The more he thought about it, the more he realized the suggestion was a lucky throw of the dice. "But if you hire a teacher, you will have more time to oversee your other charities."

"I never thought of it that way," she said slowly.

He pressed his advantage. "There are so many needs, and you are the woman whose abilities can make a difference."

Her gaze contemplated him. He smiled his most engaging smile. This was a delicate moment, and he did not want to ruin his chances. He remembered her clear generous spirit he had seen that morning, and it still lured him. He wanted her for his wife.

"You meant it at the farmyard, didn't you?" she asked, "When you said you intended to rebuild the cottage with your own funds."

"Yes," he said in a low voice. He did not want Linton to learn of his plans.

"I fear I misjudged you. I seem to do that fairly often."

He remained silent, allowing her time to reassess him. Confidence flowed within him. It would be a good marriage.

Then Linton spoke.

"Forget this talk about schools. London is where you want to be."

Sir Gerard saw the wariness flare up again in Annette's eyes. The harmonious bond, which had been forming between them, shattered like a broken goblet. To himself, he cursed his friend's exuberance while he attempted to repair the damage. "In London you would be able to learn more about how others are helping those in need."

From the corner of his eye, he saw Linton's look of disbelief, but he ignored it. Annette held his attention.

She set down her glass. "True, but that kind of trip does not require being gone for the entire Season. I could do it on my own." With those words, he knew her answer even before she told him. "I regret I must decline your generous offer of this morning. Thank you, sir."

He could not believe she chose that school over him. "You need more time to consider."

She stood. "No, I fear I do not. I appreciate the excellent dinner, but it is time for us to leave. After all, we keep country hours here in Upper Brampton."

He would not beg. Her rejection was the low point of a

day that had begun with so much sparkling promise. They bade their farewells. He fought to act the part of the gracious host.

When the door closed behind them, Sir Gerard bleakly faced the future before him. The brilliance of the morning had not accurately foretold of the day ahead. It made the forthcoming night appear darker. Linton had not only ruined the evening, he had destroyed his chance to marry an admirable woman.

Bundled warmly inside the carriage heading home, Lucille asked Annette, "Why did you refuse Sir Gerard?"

Although Annette wanted to avoid the question, she knew there would be no peace until she answered. "You heard him. I could not trust he would allow my school to continue."

"You think he would close it? He did not appear to think that way."

Annette felt the need to defend herself. "No, but he did not approve of my teaching."

"He suggested hiring a teacher," Lucille reminded her.

"True, but I like teaching. I like presenting the lessons to the children. I want to be a part of their lives."

"So you settled for the substitute of your students for your own children." The carriage bounced over a deep rut in the road, causing Lucille to gasp before continuing, "You can't teach forever. Hiring someone was a good idea."

"At least the children are mine now, if only for a little while."

Lucille would not relent in her probing. "But they aren't. When school is over, they go home to their parents.

You could have had your own. So what is the true reason you refused him?"

Annette looked out the window, pretending to see the view in the darkness outside. "I told you before he does not love me. I will not marry without love."

"I think you are afraid to discover if he does love you. Why? Do you love him?"

The question filled the night, demanding a response. She remembered his kisses and the way he always managed to confound her suppositions. Such things should irritate her, but she found them to be charming. Was that love?

"I do not know," Annette whispered.

The carriage rattled home in silence.

Chapter Twelve

Sir Gerard let Silver Shadow pick his way along the rutted, wet lane. Earlier this afternoon he had enjoyed a fast canter across his lands. He had hoped the vigorous ride would dispel the clouds of mental fog that covered days.

It had not worked.

Since Annette's rejection of his proposal nearly two weeks ago, the world appeared bleak to his gaze. Glancing around at the early March countryside, he saw only empty branches and dead leaves and grasses covering the muddy ground. The high hedges hemmed him in along this path to Hathaway Hall. Behind them birds chirped and fluttered about their business. He knew a hidden spring stirred, but the effects of winter overlaid his heart. The new season seemed to taunt him with its hope. Spring would not bloom for him.

When would he see her again? She had not gone to the last Assembly, and he had missed church on Sunday. They would meet again. Upper Brampton's society was too small for them to avoid each other forever. He wished some excuse existed for calling on her, but as of yet none had occurred to him.

Silver Shadow rounded a curve, and Sir Gerard spotted two men standing before him. Dressed in dirty clothes and wearing heavy coats, they looked unsavory.

He expected them to step aside. Instead, they moved closer to block the center of the lane. Sir Gerard reined in his horse. Silver Shadow nickered and sidestepped nervously. They were probably out-of-work miners or drovers. Such men could be dangerous.

He looked back. A third man stood there. Sir Gerard remained alert in the saddle. "Move aside, there," he commanded the two before him.

One man stepped forward to grasp Silver Shadow's bridle. Leering up, he displayed several missing teeth from his yellowed collection. "Be ye Sir Gerard Montfort?"

"Release my horse," he demanded. He tugged at the reins, but the man's grip did not break.

"I asked ye a question," the man said. His companions moved to either side of the baronet. Silver Shadow shifted edgily.

Sir Gerard felt the unease grow within him. "I told you to let go of my horse."

"Ye be right uncivil," the leader complained. "I want to know if ye be Sir Gerard Montfort?"

"What do you want?"

"So ye be him. I thought so." The man nodded in satisfaction. "We have a message for ye."

A frisson of cold, which had nothing to do with the weather, shivered down Sir Gerard's spine. "A message? From whom?"

"Seize him, boys!"

Rough hands grabbed his arms and legs to pull him

from his mount. Sir Gerard kicked Silver Shadow's sides in an effort to break through. Trapped and frightened, the horse screamed and tried to rear.

Sir Gerard began to slide backwards. He fought to stay astride. One of the horse's hooves hit an attacker's leg. The man cursed and fell to his knees, but did not let go of the reins.

Then Sir Gerard was hauled from his horse. He would have fallen to the ground, except for the tight grip two of the men retained on his arms. Freed from the crowd, Silver Shadow galloped for home and his stall.

Breathing heavily, the leader stepped back. "The message is from Mortimer Wallace. He don't like it when he ain't paid."

Sir Gerard tried unsuccessfully to break free. "Wallace was paid what I owed him."

The man shook his head. "He says ye be a week overdue. He wants his money back."

"I do not owe it to him." With difficulty, Sir Gerard swallowed his angry words and tried another tack. "Let's be reasonable about this. Money is the whole issue here."

"I be a reasonable man. What did you have in mind?"

"Bill here's a thinker," the man on his right commented.

Sir Gerard attempted to use his vaunted charm. In a conversational tone that did not display his inner tension, he said, "Well, Bill, I have a proposition for you. Wallace hired you, so you work for money."

"Who don't?" the leader grumbled.

The men's grip did not loosen, but Sir Gerard sensed that they were listening. "I am quite willing to pay all three of you to ride off, and we pretend this meeting never happened."

Bill eyed his prisoner with suspicion. "How can ye pay us if ye don't have no money for Wallace?"

"I never said I do not have any money. Only that I do not owe any to that money-lender." He watched Bill closely. Would his gamble to escape succeed?

Bill shook his head. "Ye are good, sir. I'll grant ye that. Ye almost convinced me. But Wallace, he pays us regular. Ye would likely turn us over to the magistrate."

"No, I won't," Sir Gerard promised in desperation.

It was too late.

The first blow struck him in the stomach, forcing the air from his lungs. The next hit his cheek with a loud crack. He struggled to free himself. The fists continued to assail him, until his knees buckled. He let his weight sag against his captors' arms. He prayed, *Let it be over soon.*

"Now, Jack it is very important that you behave correctly towards the baronet," Annette admonished the boy sitting beside her in the landau.

"I will, Miss Courtney," he assured her for probably the tenth time.

She knew Jack would conduct himself properly. After all, it was his academic ability and respectful behavior that had originally led her to ask Sir Gerard to help her protégé. In the month since, no offers had come Jack's way. It was high time to remind the baronet.

As she drove along the drive towards Hathaway Hall, she admitted to herself Jack was not her only reason for visiting. She wanted to see Sir Gerard again.

She had turned down his proposal, but he was not so easily banished from her memory. The contradictions within him intrigued her. She liked order in her world. So why did someone who confused her still attract her? Perhaps by seeing him again, she could understand why she could not forget him.

The rattle of the landau and the clomp of her horse's hooves on the wet road blocked any sounds of nature. When her carriage turned a curve, the sight before her caused her to gasp with astonishment, even as she pulled back on the reins.

Two men supported Sir Gerard between them, while a third hit him. The baronet's head drooped. He made no effort to struggle.

In a flash, Annette dropped the reins and jumped down from the landau. "Stop it! What are you doing?"

With his fist still cocked, the man turned to her. "Ye stay out of this, ma'am."

"I most certainly will not."

She saw him hit Sir Gerard again, and she forgot everything except that she could not allow this beating to continue. From the landau, she snatched up her driving whip. She seldom used it on her horse, never being in that much of a hurry to arrive at her destination. Yet she had no compunction about attacking the men before her.

The first strike of the whip landed soundly on the man's back. With a curse, he faced her. "This be our business. Ye stay out of it."

Annette's answer was another crack, this time at his legs. The man jumped back too late to avoid the whip's sting.

"Get her," he growled.

The others released Sir Gerard, who dropped into the mud and lay still. Her heart stopped within her at his piteous condition, but she could not attend to him. Standing beside the horse's head, she watched the three men spread out before her. A fast swing of the whip at their legs kept them a respectable distance away.

"You men get out of here," she commanded with the authority of years of ordering others to do her bidding.

"Ye wanted to be involved in our business, so we'll let ye."

She snaked the whip at the man on the right. He leaped backwards, slipped in the wet mud, and fell. Another crack kept him from rising. Two remained.

At that moment Jack appeared behind the assailant on her left. Her student held a thick branch obviously snatched from the forest ground. With a satisfying thump, he brought it down on the man's head. The attacker fell as if chopped by an ax. Jack gave him no chance to stand up and whacked him about the head and shoulders.

The sudden loss of his support caused the leader in the middle to pause. He glanced at his companions at his feet and then at Sir Gerard, who was struggling to sit up. "We're off. We're done here anyways."

Holding the whip ready, Annette watched him step back. She allowed the man in the mud to get up. Jack moved away from his target, but held his branch like the ax he was more familiar with.

Stumbling and swearing, the men regrouped themselves safely out of reach. The leader looked as if he might reconsider leaving. Annette gave a sharp crack with the whip to send them on their way.

She waited until they were out of sight before she turned her attention to Sir Gerard. She dropped the whip by his side and ordered, "Jack, keep a watch out for them in case they come back."

The baronet was sitting up, but there was a dazed look on his battered face. From a cut at his temple, a thin line of blood snaked down his cheek. His skin was beginning to swell and turn purple.

She was glad she had used her whip on his attackers. Fiercely glad. Kneeling beside him, she asked, "How badly did they hurt you?"

"I'm still alive . . . I think."

The fact that he could still attempt humor after what he had just been through made her giggle with an edge of hysteria. She pulled a handkerchief from her sleeve to dab at the blood on his face, but her hand shook. Reaction was setting in.

He took her hand in his. "That was a foolish thing you did."

She read the gratitude and admiration in his swelling eyes and was even more discomfited. "I was so surprised I did not know what to do," she babbled. "I did not even think." She freed her hand to tend to him.

"I am grateful—Ow!" he exclaimed when she pressed the handkerchief too hard against one of his wounds.

"I'm sorry." She pulled her hand back from his face. "Who were those men? What did they want?"

"They were from Wallace, the money-lender," he explained at her puzzled look. "He and I had a difference of opinion about some money he claims I owe."

"But I paid that."

"Only the first installment. He is demanding the balance to be paid off. I refused. I will pay the second installment when due." He laughed bitterly, winced, and touched his cut lip. "This is the result."

"The magistrate will hear about this," she declared. "That money-lender should be jailed."

"I don't think it will be Wallace who ends up behind

bars. A man like him has more incarnations than the Devil. Only his hirelings will suffer."

Looking at his battered face, Annette felt her heart clench. If she had not driven by when she did . . .

With difficulty, she tore her gaze away from him. "We need to get you taken care of. Can you make it into my landau?"

"I would rather ride than walk back to Hathaway Hall." He began to struggle to his feet.

Annette stood to help him up, but now it was her own legs that wobbled beneath her. "Three of them," she said. "There were three of them."

She swayed as the fear of what she had done overtook her. How could she even have considered taking on so many men?

Sir Gerard grasped her about the shoulders to steady her. "You are the bravest woman I know, Annette. With gratitude and admiration, I salute you."

He kissed her. Because his lips were swollen, his touch was light against her mouth. It only lasted a brief moment. A salute just like he stated, but it was as if it sparked an explosion of realization within her.

She loved him.

Seeing him hurt made her understand how much she could have lost. Despite his infuriating manners, despite his gambling background, and despite his interference in her school, she loved him. Or perhaps because of all those reasons. She did not know, and now was not the time to ponder it.

He needed her help.

She could no longer refuse him anything.

Somehow, with Jack's support, she managed to get the

baronet into the landau. He filled more than half of the seat.

With a rueful smile, she told the boy, "There is no room for you. I am afraid you will have to walk home."

Jack nodded in understanding. In the fight, he had lost his cap and now his brown hair stood up like stalks of wheat.

Sir Gerard said, "Introduce me to this brave lad who helped us."

"This is my student, Jack Farmer. I was intending to present him to you this afternoon."

"I wish we could have met under more favorable circumstances," Sir Gerard said.

"Me, too, sir."

"He is the boy for whom I hoped you would be able to find a position," Annette explained.

Understanding, Sir Gerard glanced at her. "Another request, Miss Courtney?"

"A repeat of one," she reminded him.

He nodded to Jack. "I hear you are a good student."

"Miss Courtney makes me try to be one, sir."

"Miss Courtney makes people do a lot of things they had not originally intended," Sir Gerard commented. "In this instance, she is correct. A lad with your courage deserves a chance. Perhaps my steward could use a bright helper."

The boy tried not to squirm under the praise. "Thank you, sir. It means a lot to me." He vigorously shook the baronet's hand, not understanding the fixed grimace on Sir Gerard's face when he did so.

"Go on home, Jack, but be careful. Those men are probably long gone, but they could still be lurking about,"

Annette said. "Tell your folks about being the steward's clerk. They will be very proud of you."

"Yes, ma'am. Thank you, sir." Whistling cheerfully, Jack swaggered back down the lane.

Annette picked up the reins and started her horse forward. "You should have told me Wallace still demanded more money."

"None of my requests for the money succeeded, and you had already paid one installment on my loan. A man wants to retain some pride."

Letting the horse walk at its own pace, she could not keep her gaze from straying towards Sir Gerard. He lay back as much as one could in such a small carriage. His hands rested on his legs. Mud covered him everywhere. The sleeve to his wool coat was torn, and the bruising was darkening his face. Her heart squeezed with sympathy to see such a man so hurt.

"I guess I did not fully understand the threat," she said softly. "Will they be back?"

He shifted in an effort to find a more comfortable position, causing the whole carriage to sway. "I doubt it, but I will visit the magistrate. A letter to Wallace warning of the danger of a repeat attack would not come amiss, either."

The carriage hit a rut, and Sir Gerard groaned at the jouncing.

"I apologize for that," she said. "I will try to go slower, but I need to get you home to care."

"Do not worry about me," he replied. "I will recover just fine."

She wondered if her heart would recover. She never expected to fall in love—and certainly not with such a man. Now she wished she had not refused his proposal. But in the unlikely event, he offered again, could she accept?

She loved him.

He did not love her.

She had always prided herself upon her talent to manage any problem, but never had she faced a situation like this one. She would give anything to protect him from any further threat. He needed her, and she would use all her abilities to help him. When the carriage reached the front entrance of Hathaway Hall, she knew what she must do.

The manor servants were in an uproar. Silver Shadow had galloped back to the stable, agitated and lathered. A search party was in the process of being organized when the landau pulled up to the front door. A hot bath was ordered, and the baronet placed under the anxious care of his servants. Once she saw that his needs were being met, she turned the landau towards Upper Brampton village.

At the solicitor's office, she said, "I want to give the money to Sir Gerard."

Chapter Thirteen

Sir Gerard was stunned by the news the solicitor had brought yesterday afternoon. Apparently out of the blue, Annette was returning his fortune to him.

"But why?" he had asked the solicitor.

Mr. Keller shrugged his shoulders in helpless ignorance.

Only Annette could tell him the reason.

So here he stood on her doorstep. He knew he did not present his usual elegant appearance for calling. The shaving glass that morning still reflected the purpling of his face. It was starting to yellow at the edges of the bruises. At least this time when she saw him, his clothes would not be torn and covered in mud. He would have been much worse off, if not for her. His mouth tightened grimly at the memory.

Yesterday afternoon, in addition to the solicitor, the magistrate had called at Sir Gerard's request. The baronet hoped to make life very difficult for one Mortimer Wallace. And now he had the funds to do so.

But first he needed to speak with Annette.

Her maid ushered him into the simply furnished drawing room. Annette and her companion were sewing. He noticed Mrs. Downes whisked hers out of sight under a pillow, while Annette displayed no such signs of embarrassment at the plain sewing she worked upon. She greeted him and sent for tea.

Seating himself on the proffered chair, Sir Gerard gazed at the woman he had once hated, then admired, and finally proposed to. She sat erect, with her needle passing in and out of the muslin. For the first time, a spinster's cap now rested on her soft brown hair. It declared her social status as permanently set upon the shelf, and it saddened him. He liked her—a great deal.

"What are you working on?" he asked.

In her forthright manner, she replied, "This is a shirt for the church to distribute to the poor."

"You are always busy for others," he said. "You have a generous spirit."

"Thank you, sir."

Mrs. Downes offered him a cup of tea and the plate of cakes, and he selected one. He did not know how to broach the topic that most concerned him. None of his London manners had prepared him for such a situation. So he decided to take a page from Annette's own book and be direct.

"I had a most interesting call yesterday," he commented.

"Who was it?" Mrs. Downes asked.

Taking a sip of his tea, he noticed the rhythm of Annette's sewing barely slowed. "Mr. Keller, the solicitor. He brought me some very unusual news." Neither woman said anything. What he was about to say was surely not a surprise to them. "I have gained control of my uncle's money. What I wonder is why?"

Mrs. Downes looked at Annette, who took several more stitches before saying, "You must be very pleased to have obtained that which you have sought for so long."

"Yes, I am," he said. "But why now?"

"It was only justice that it should go with the estate it should serve."

"I will not deny that I am glad to have it. Nor do I have a quarrel with the trust set up to maintain the school. It is a good charity."

Annette set down her sewing, a look of relief spreading over her face. "I feared you might begrudge that money. Is that not why you called?"

Surprise filled him. "Begrudge that well-run school?" He winked at her. "Never! It produces such excellent students as the lad who will now be assisting my steward."

She smiled. "That is an excellent position for Jack."

"He earned it." Sir Gerard set down his teacup and leaned forward. "Miss Courtney, I could never resent your school. It is too important to you, and you are doing such good work. I only wonder that it can function on the small sum you requested."

"I did not wish to be greedy."

"Your generous nature could never be considered greedy. I will increase the endowment. Prices are going up all the time."

"It is you who are generous." Her approving gaze rested upon him, and he felt like he had just been knighted.

Perhaps a marriage between them based upon feelings of affection could have worked. He would never know. Spotting the white cap on her head, a twinge of sadness nipped at his heart.

To banish it, he said, "You also kept none of the money for yourself."

"What?" Mrs. Downes sputtered and set her cup down with a loud rattle. Plainly, this news surprised her. "Annette, you didn't!"

"It was not mine to keep," Annette answered.

"My uncle willed it all to you. The money was yours for whatever you wished."

She shook her head. "I learned Sir Nigel only bequeathed the fortune to me in order to spite you. I could no longer be a party to such cruelty."

A strong emotion flared in her eyes, but her gaze returned to her sewing too quickly for him to analyze it. Still, that glimpse into her soul shook him. There was more here to restoring his fortune than simple charity. What emotion had he spotted?

"You need an income to support yourself," he argued. "I intend to set up an annuity for you."

"You are not obliged to do so," she said. "All the money is yours to spend."

"The money you kept is to fund the school," he pointed out. "There is nothing held back for yourself."

"I regard that differently. I often requested the funds from Sir Nigel to start the school, but he always refused me."

He pursed his lips. "You are not above a little revenge, I see."

A darker shade of red crept up her cheeks, causing him to smile at her humanness. "The children need an education so badly," she said.

"They will receive one with you managing, and my uncle pays for it in the end. The annuity will prevent you from struggling to survive." He thought he was beginning to understand why she had returned the money. His uncle's spite had recoiled upon his wishes. Refusing to support the old miser's plans, she funded the school and returned the money. If she kept an annuity, it would mean doing what Sir Nigel had planned. Sir Gerard sought to reassure her. "The annuity is my gift for you. You can use it to fund any charities you want."

"Oh, Annette," Mrs. Downes interjected. "It could be so helpful. Must we return to our former way of life?"

Annette's face softened when she looked at her companion.

Sir Gerard pressed his advantage. "As you well know, an annuity for you would be no burden upon the estate." He added the clincher. "You cannot deny your companion an easier life."

Quietly to herself, Annette said, "I need to be fair to Lucille, too." She turned to him. "I will not refuse an annuity from you. Your generosity is most welcome."

Satisfied he had learned what he wanted to know, Sir Gerard leaned back in his chair to drink his tea and enjoy the remainder of the call. "Now that that is settled, I have some news for you. I am planning to head for London in the next couple of days."

Annette's stitching stilled. "London? I thought you were going to stay in Upper Brampton."

"Of course I will be visiting here, but the Season will start in a few weeks. I intend to enjoy it this year."

Dismay filled her face, and she crumpled her sewing between her hands. "But what about your plans for your tenants? You talked of redoing the cottages."

He smiled. Her concern for others was one of the traits he liked best about her. "I do not need to be here to build them with my own two hands. Carpenters are quite capable."

"But someone needs to oversee them."

"Surely my steward will be quite capable as well. After all, he now has a smart lad to assist him." He winked at her, but no answering sparkle responded from Annette.

She frowned at him. "No steward can replace the eye of the owner. You should be here."

Under her disapproval, he shifted. The upholstered chair was no longer comfortable. "I will be back. Certainly you did not expect me to bury myself here in Upper Brampton forever."

Her gaze did not waver. "No, some trips to London are to be expected. I only fear an absentee landlord. When he is gone, he can easily forget those who depend upon him so heavily."

Her distrust upset him. "I will not forget them." He set his teacup down on the table with such strength that it clattered on the saucer. "Even if I did, I am sure letters from you would arrive reminding me."

"If necessary, I will follow your suggestion and send those messages." He heard the implied threat in her tone.

The cakes and tea no longer tasted sweet to him. Everything was soured. What had happened to his bright outlook? He stood. "Thank you for the tea and the words of advice. I must leave now to prepare for my trip."

"When shall we expect you to be back?" she asked.

Annoyed, he bit off the words of his answer. "The Season lasts into June. I expect to enjoy every minute of it. Then, if I am invited to a house party, I intend to go. Does my schedule meet with your approval, Miss Courtney?"

Very calmly, she replied, "I only wondered when we might see you again."

"I shall be certain to call upon you when I return." He bowed to her formally, nodded farewell to Mrs. Downes, and strode from the room.

Outside, he clamped his hat onto his head with more force than necessary. Yanking Silver Shadow's reins free from the fence, he mounted and headed for home.

"That woman could drive a saint to drink," he told the horse.

For the first time, he had some sympathy for his uncle. No wonder Sir Nigel would avoid seeing Annette. Right now, he did not want to meet her again, either. She had no authority to approve or disapprove his plans. Who did she think she was? Calling him an absentee landlord in such a disdainful tone of voice. Those cottages would be built. He would keep that promise. He would prove everyone's judgment about him wrong.

Sir Gerard nudged Silver Shadow's sides, urging him to a greater speed. He could not wait to reach London and revel in its every pastime of pleasure.

The sound of retreating hoofbeats resonated in the very quiet drawing room. Annette heard them fade, and wondered how she could have so misjudged him. He seemed to prove himself a wastrel at every opportunity. Where was the man she saw beneath the social façade? Where was the man from the fire who cared about his tenants? The one who offered Jack a chance? Where had he gone?

Lucille's whisper broke the strained silence.

"I'm so sorry."

"There is no need to be." Annette picked up her crumpled sewing from her lap. Her hands trembled so, she hid them under the fabric. "I have nothing to regret."

She only wished that statement was true. She regretted lots of things. Chief among them was that Sir Gerard was not the man she wanted him to be. Yet, she did not regret her love. No, she told herself fiercely, love should never be a cause for regret. Pasting a broad smile on her face, she said, "I am certain he will have a wonderful time in London."

"He belongs here!" Lucille declared with more intensity than was her wont. "With you."

Her friend's defense warmed the chill in Annette's heart. "We cannot make him do what he does not want, but I appreciate your thoughtfulness. You are a good woman."

"So are you." Lucille pulled her sewing out from its hiding place under the pillow. "After all, you gave him back that money. He has no right to go off and spend it in that city."

Genuine amusement trickled through Annette, making her more grateful to the other woman. "Of course he can. It is his money now."

"You should have attached strings to it," Lucille grumbled.

Annette could not help chuckling. Although her heart feared the times she shared with Sir Gerard were over, she still possessed the tried-and-true comfort of her friend. "The only stipulation I attached was the funding for my school. I need to concentrate on that."

"You deserve more."

"He will give us an annuity. The school will keep me plenty busy." She noticed Lucille had not restarted her sewing. To set the example of how she meant to go on, Annette picked up her needle. "After all, it is the achievement of my dream. Apparently going to London and partaking of the social scene is his."

Her friend started to protest, but a stern glance from Annette commanded her silence on the topic. Ignoring it, Lucille said, "I don't see why. He has lived there for years already."

With great care, Annette set a tiny stitch in the fabric. "It is his chance to shine among the *ton*. He has long craved their admiration."

"Everyone looked up to him here." Lucille's needle remained unmoving in her hand. "Besides, London is where he got into so much trouble with his gambling."

A bolt of dread shot through Annette. With an unerring aim, her friend had voiced the one fear that Annette did not want to confront.

"I am sure he is through with that," she said in a small voice. "He did not gamble when he was here."

"He did not have the money."

"Oh, hush, Lucille." The other woman was expressing every argument she herself would have used. Annette did not like being on the receiving end of such logic when it was the emotion of love that had ruled her decision. She could not marry without love on her beloved's side. Instead, she had given him his heart's desire, but she did not intend to inform the world—or Lucille—of the fact.

"It was a grave injustice that the money ever came to me. Sir Nigel did it out of spite," Annette said. "I wanted to set things right."

"Marriage would have set things right." The other woman cast a knowing glance at Annette.

"That was an impossible solution. I told you so many

times." Looking up from her work, she pleaded, "I truly do not wish to continue this conversation."

Her friend's face softened. "I understand. You have suffered a great disappointment."

Setting aside her neglected sewing, Lucille gathered up the tea things and returned to the kitchen.

After the door swung shut behind her companion, Annette stopped her pretense of sewing and looked over at the chair where Sir Gerard had sat. She could almost see his presence still there. The male scent of horse and shaving soap lingered, causing her to inhale deeply, eager to hold onto something of him for as long as she could. If he ever returned, he would not be the man she had known.

Lucille called the feeling inside disappointment, but Annette thought the hollow darkness within deserved a far stronger name than disappointment. It was despair that beat at her heart like a moth frantically seeking the light.

London lay very far away, and there were many bright temptations to change a man. Besides the gambling, there were the women, so sophisticated and brilliantly beautiful. Annette knew she could never compete against them. One of them would be chosen his bride. Someday she would even call on the lady. Someday.

Her hands tightened, further crumpling the muslin work on her lap. Why was her love not enough for marriage? Why had she refused him when she had the chance to snatch up his offer and make him hers forever?

Because he would not have been hers. A tear started to trickle down her face, and she hurriedly wiped it away. This overwrought distress would never do.

She had to face the facts. A marriage based solely on

her love would have left her constantly seeking signs of affection from her husband. She would have been like an active puppy, appreciated occasionally, but never respected like an equal partner. She could not live in such a marriage. Eventually her love would have died from a lack of appreciation.

Annette smoothed the work on her lap. She had made her choice in life. Losing Sir Gerard was the consequence. Always before, she had faced life's setbacks directly and moved forward. She could—no, she must—do the same this time.

With grim determination, Annette set a stitch along the seam she was sewing. She made another one. Then another one.

She had her school. Those children were going to learn. It was the only mission that remained to her. She would teach them.

And someday, she would graciously call upon the new Lady Montfort.

The private coach rattled on towards London. Inside, Sir Gerard and Linton bounced around like dice at a gambling table.

Despite the rough treatment, Linton sighed with satisfaction. "I, for one, am glad to be leaving here. No offense meant to your home and all that, but it was a mighty quiet time."

Grabbing the strap to steady himself, Sir Gerard said, "Quiet? I thought there was always something happening."

"The Assemblies were only once a week, with occasional dinner parties where the country maidens were displayed for our benefit." Linton shuddered. "It was *not* a social life."

"You will get that in London."

"Yes, and am I glad to be headed there."

The anticipation in his friend's voice reflected the excitement within Sir Gerard. "At last," he agreed, "no more living as the necessary extra man for hostesses or working to survive by training horses. At last I am my own man."

Linton punched his friend on the shoulder. "I am grateful you covered my debts, so I could join you."

"We have been through too much together for me to leave you behind," Sir Gerard said.

The carriage jolted over a series of deep ruts, nearly tossing its passengers from their seats. The coachman was obeying his master's orders to make Godspeed for London.

When he had recovered his breath, Linton asked, "Did you ever find out why the spinster returned the money?"

Annoyance shot through Sir Gerard. "You will call her Miss Courtney. She deserves your respect."

Linton raised his eyebrows, but complied. "Miss Courtney surrendered it so easily. I wonder why."

"I found out. She finally agreed to the justice of my claim." He did not want to remember his final call upon Annette. That glimpse of deep emotion he had caught upon her face still bothered him. As a very righteous woman, she could not allow such an injustice to continue. Many times since that visit he had reassured himself thusly, but somehow, he remained unconvinced.

Linton chuckled. "You were lucky to escape without marriage."

"Yes, lucky," Sir Gerard muttered. He did not want to think of that good fortune. With determination, he grinned to his friend. "I hope London is ready for us with wine, women, and song."

Sir Gerard buried the twinge of regret pricking inside him and joined Linton in a rousing sailors' melody that would have been banned from the drawing room of any hostess.

The coach rattled towards London.

Chapter Fourteen

Annette wondered if the spring air was to blame for causing her students to act up. The early April weather still possessed a nip, but its breezes burgeoned with the promise of future blooms. The same energy infected the schoolchildren.

More and more they shifted restlessly on their benches. Although she could not fault Sir Gerard, things at the school seemed to become difficult soon after he left for London over three weeks ago.

"Tom, you can read this passage." She put as much encouragement for the nervous student into her voice. "These are all words you have studied."

With great concentration, the boy wrinkled his brow and pointed his finger at the word in the Bible. "He went down to J-J-J . . ." His voice trailed off, and he looked to her for help.

"Joppa," she said. Her smile felt tight on her face.

"Joppa." Tom struggled on. "Found a ship going to Tar-Tar-Tar—" The boy looked up. "I'd like to go on a ship. I want to be a cabin boy and fight the French."

Annette tried to steer his attention back to his assignment, but the prospect of sailing tempted him more than the story of Jonah and the big whale. She saw the rest of the class no longer even listened to the slow reading. In fact, John had just tweaked Molly's braid. Molly retaliated with a push. Indignant whispers and pushing ensued.

With a sigh, Annette sent Tom back to his seat and administered discipline to the restive children.

Arithmetic fared no better. The simple addition and subtraction she had drilled into their heads seemed to have melted with the winter snows. Blank stares met her efforts at word problems. As for penmanship, why chickens scratched more neatly in the barnyard! Annette shook her head in dismay.

Even Jack, the one student of whom she was so proud, appeared disinterested in the weekly lessons she taught him after school at her home.

"Were you able to read the chapter in that history book?" she asked him. They were seated together on the couch in her drawing room.

He shrugged. "I started to, Miss Courtney, but it weren't interesting at all."

She had assumed knights and battles would attract a boy. "It is the history of England. You should know it."

"But what does it have to do with being a steward?" he asked.

"Knowledge of history is required of an educated man." She opened the book to the chapter and thrust it at him. "Please read this passage to me, and then we will discuss it."

Jack stumbled through the reading and the following discussion, although it was she who did most of the talking.

Afterwards, through the window, she watched him run

up the street for home. She let out a long, slow breath, and her shoulders slumped as she sat down again on her chair.

To be honest, she knew her discontent was not the children's fault. They acted no differently from when she started the school.

She amended that thought. Maybe a bit more restless due to the seasonal change, but their antics had not worn on her the way they did now. Now she saw only the disciplining she must administer, not the nurturing of blossoming learning. She had her school, but her joy in it had vanished when her dream had changed.

Now the dream of a family of her own surged within her, only this time she knew who wore the wanted face of her husband. She had had her chance when he had proposed, but she had refused. Without love from him, this dream too would have withered. She would never gain her heart's true desire, but she must not wallow in discontent. She punched a pillow into shape and arranged it in the corner of the couch. Thoughts of the baronet must be banished. The school was enough for her. She would make it so.

London suited Sir Gerard just as he always dreamed it would. He found a small, yet elegant, apartment for himself, but he was seldom at home in it. The clubs, the parties, and the balls all beckoned. He filled his days and a good portion of his nights with the pleasures his money bought.

One of the most pleasant was his interview with Mortimer Wallace. Sir Gerard summoned the money-lender to his chambers. He was careful not to rise in a greeting when the man was admitted.

"Baronet Westcourt." Wallace bowed.

"I am glad you came." Sir Gerard leaned back in his chair. He was pleased to notice the fine sheen of perspiration covering the other man's face. The climb up the stairs must have winded him.

"You said it was urgent." The money-lender glanced at an empty chair, but Sir Gerard did not offer it to him. He intended the man to realize who was in command of this interview.

"Yes, I have two items to deal with you." Sir Gerard pulled himself upright in his chair. Beneath his tightened grip, he felt the roughness of its brocaded upholstery. "First, you will shortly receive a draft on my bank which will pay off the balance of my loan to you."

A wide insincere smile creased Wallace's face. "That is no longer necessary, sir. I have learned of your good luck in gaining your uncle's fortune. I am quite willing to abide by the original terms. You can pay the installments—and interest—as we agreed."

"I no longer agree." Sir Gerard stood and moved closer to let his height tower over the money-lender. "The contract no longer exists between us. In fact, I have contacted the magistrates, both in Wiltshire and here in London, to investigate an attack made upon me."

"I am very sorry to hear—"

"When the culprits are found, they will testify as to whom ordered that attack."

Wallace spread out his plump hands in an ingratiating manner. "Surely that is not necessary. You survived, and I am getting my loan repaid."

Sir Gerard's gaze bore into the other man. "You would not want such ruffians running free. Law and order must be upheld."

The wet sheen on the money-lender's face appeared

even thicker. A drop rolled down his chin. "Of course, the law must deal with criminals, but you and I can forget any unpleasantness between us. Should it become necessary, I would be happy to lend you any further sums."

Smiling so that his teeth showed, Sir Gerard said, "I will not be borrowing from you again, but I eagerly anticipate prosecuting *all* of those involved in my attack. I now have the money to do so."

Wallace visibly trembled. He cleared his throat. "Surely that is more action than is needed."

"Oh, but it is very necessary." To send him on his way, Sir Gerard distastefully took the money-lender's arm and propelled him out the door.

The man started to sputter. Sir Gerard shut the door on him and felt an immense satisfaction that was worth the revulsion of inviting that disgusting man into his rooms. He was grateful to Annette, both for saving him physically from that man's attack and giving him the financial means for revenge.

A little smile crossed his lips as he wondered what she was doing. Probably teaching those students. She was determined to drill knowledge into those boys and girls, whether they wanted it or not. He was a little surprised at not receiving any letter from her by now. The steward must be following his orders to listen to her suggestions. From the dry, factual reports Sir Gerard received, he knew estate matters were progressing well. Somehow the prospect that he was not needed at Hathaway Hall depressed him.

Two weeks after his encounter with Wallace, Linton stopped by one evening. Sir Gerard had just poured two glasses of a smuggled French brandy for Linton and himself. He relaxed in the chair to enjoy it and a bit of conversation. The two men raised their cups in silent toast to each other.

After tasting his drink, Linton said, "That is a fine brandy. You can certainly afford the best now."

"The journey was not easy. You were there through it all, for which I am grateful." Sir Gerard felt the brandy tingle as he swallowed. In the same manner, Annette's memory tingled at his brain, causing him to miss her. He thought of her more often than he expected.

"I certainly am grateful you paid off those debts of mine," Linton said. "It enabled me to return to London."

Sir Gerard grinned at his friend with fondness. "I had to. What would the Season be like without you by my side?" Linton had stuck with him through the bad times, and now he wanted his friend to enjoy the good ones. "Here's to good times ahead." He raised his glass in another toast.

"To good times."

They both sipped their drinks. Then Linton said, "I want to keep the good times, but I have run into a slight problem."

"What is it?" Sir Gerard waited to learn how he could help his friend.

The other man did not look at him. He studied the rich amber color of the brandy before clearing his throat. "There is no easy way to say it. I need some more money."

"More money!" The request astounded Sir Gerard. "I thought I paid off your debts when we arrived here. Did we overlook some?"

"No, you paid them all."

"Then what happened?"

"You know how it is," Linton explained. "Society is expensive."

Sir Gerard nodded. "True. Yet this is only the end of April. I just paid off everything when we got here in March."

"You sound like a money-lender yourself," Linton muttered, and gulped a large swallow of his brandy.

Sir Gerard stiffened at the insult before forcing himself to ignore it. Linton was upset over his finances. Having been in such a situation more times than he cared to remember, Sir Gerard resolved not to treat his friend in the same humiliating manner.

"Forgive me," he said. "Your request surprised me. Tell me what you need."

Linton bestowed a genial smile upon him. "I knew you would understand. You are a true friend."

Raising his glass in acknowledgment of the compliment, Sir Gerard asked, "How much do you need?"

"About eight hundred pounds!"

Sir Gerard choked on his brandy and began to cough. Linton leapt to his feet and pounded his friend on the back.

When Sir Gerard could speak, though his throat was raw from the coughing fit, he asked weakly, "Did you say eight hundred pounds?"

Linton studied his friend with concern before being satisfied he was recovered. He sat down again. "That is about what I estimate I need right now to cover the most pressing ones."

"You mean there are more?"

"Dash it all," Linton complained. "You are starting to sound like the pater when I ask him for an increase in my allowance."

Sir Gerard had forgotten about his friend's allowance. Since Sir Nigel had never granted him one, he tended to overlook the existence of Linton's, yet it had sustained the two of them during the lean times. It was this past obligation that caused him to repay Linton's debts.

"What happened to your allowance?" he asked. "Did your father not pay it at the quarter?" March was barely a month passed.

Linton squirmed under this questioning. "Yes, he paid it."

"You already spent that, too?"

The man shot him an angry look. "I do not have to account for every penny to you."

An answering anger began to build within Sir Gerard. "You do if you expect me to fund you."

"I thought you were my friend."

"I am, and I remember how you stood by me. But this is an outrageous request."

"It takes a lot of money to make your mark in society— as you should know."

To steady himself, Sir Gerard took another sip of his drink. "I do know that, but I also have plans for my fortune. There are so many things I want to do with Hathaway Hall and the estate farms. I do not intend to waste the money."

Linton's eyes narrowed. "You sound just like that spinster Miss Courtney. You used to have different ideas before you went to Upper Brampton."

Slowly Sir Gerard shook his head. "No, I always anticipated the day I would take over the title and could restore the estate."

"If that is true, then why did you bother returning to

London? You should have been content to stay in that backwater countryside."

"Because I also wanted to be a part of society. You know that."

Linton glared bitterly. "All I know is I need eight hundred pounds. Rather than go to a money-lender, I thought I could count on my *friend*."

"A friend or a convenient source of the ready?"

"It's the last time." Linton's eyes were wide with desperation. "I won't ask you for money ever again. I promise."

Sir Gerard looked at Linton with regret. He was a good friend, and they had been through much together, but Sir Gerard knew that the last promise was a lie. He could not keep funding the man's extravagant spending. Not if he wanted to proceed with his own plans for taking care of those whom depended upon the estate. "I cannot pay your debts this time."

Linton jumped to his feet. "A fine friend you turned out to be. As soon as you get the money, you turn out to be a miser just like your uncle."

The insult hurt. Sir Gerard also stood. "I am not a miser. I do spend money, but wisely, not foolishly."

"I am not a fool." Linton was breathing, heavily. "Or maybe I was to ever consider you my friend. But no longer."

He spun on his heel and stamped from the room. The door slamming behind him signaled the end of their friendship.

Despite the loss of Linton's companionship, London still suited Sir Gerard. He liked having such acclaimed beauties as Miss Lydia Holbrook in his arms when he danced at a rout. Last Season, this blue-eyed, well-dowered girl would not have even acknowledged him. This Season, he had the supper dance with her while her mother nodded with approval. The change in status pleased him very much.

He held her chair for her as she sat down, and he sat on the chair beside her. A choice selection of the delicacies were arrayed on their plates. Cold ham and crab crowded the lobster patties, while a fluffy roll edged the cut pineapple and orange chunks.

"Thank you, sir." Miss Holbrook batted her eyelashes flirtatiously at him. "This food looks very good."

He smiled at her, noticing the smooth creaminess of her cheek. Her hands were encased in white kid gloves, so he could not determine if they were work-roughened. There was never any question of Annette's hands being applied to work. He frowned at the thought. Why had he remembered that?

"Is something wrong?" Miss Holbrook asked.

"No, just an errant thought." With determination, he smiled again at her.

"I hope it was not an unpleasant one."

"How could a man think of anything unpleasant when he is with you?"

"You are too kind." She simpered at him but did not blush.

After all, her shyness at the compliment was only the practiced gesture of an experienced London beauty. Unlike Annette, whose every emotion and action was based on reality and candor.

He started to frown again, but stopped himself in time. Why did thoughts of Annette intrude? Here he was in the company of one of the Toasts, and he kept remembering a plain, outspoken spinster from the Wiltshire countryside. What was wrong with him?

"Tell me, Miss Holbrook, do you ever think about the poor?"

She blinked at him.

He berated himself. Now, what made him blurt out such a question? Those memories of Annette were addling his brain.

"The poor?" she repeated. "You wish to talk about the poor?"

In for a penny, in for a pound. He put on an expression of interest and discovered he did want to know the girl's opinion. "Yes, do you ever do charity work for them?"

Rallying from her surprise, she smiled flirtatiously at him. "Why, Sir Gerard. You know a young girl like myself cannot visit such dreadful places. Although I do feel *so* sorry for them."

"You have a kind nature," he said.

She smiled at him, her head held at an angle so he could notice her large blue eyes. "It just breaks my heart when I see them begging." She paused, waiting for his next compliment.

He responded mechanically, "Such a scene should never intrude upon the gaze of your lovely eyes. Only beauty."

"It is sad to see." Miss Holbrook pushed her food around on her plate with her fork and began to expound on the topic. "They should be working. It is only their laziness that keeps them in such poverty."

His gaze sharpened upon her. "Do you think so? Perhaps work is not available."

Her laugh trilled out in a carefully practiced melody. "You are such a tease. Of course there is work."

He did not react to her coquetry. Somehow, after knowing Annette, the topic of poverty did not seem one for frivolity. What had possessed him to start such a conversation at a rout? Of course, Annette could have talked a whole lecture on the needs of the local people. Broad theories had no place on her list of specific village needs.

"I could never argue with a lovely lady," he said. "But perhaps the wages they earn are not enough for them to live on."

She blinked her eyes, plainly not understanding his earnestness.

He smiled as he stood to escort her back to her chaperone. Yet inwardly, he rebuked himself. Miss Holbrook was only a young girl with no understanding of the world outside her protected circle. A very pretty girl, she only seemed so shallow when compared to Annette. It was not Miss Holbrook's fault that she was not the woman he wanted.

At the thought, Sir Gerard paused, causing his companion to look at him in puzzlement.

"Is something wrong?" she asked.

"No," he answered distractedly, trying to understand that wayward thought. The woman he wanted? Annette? What was he thinking of? His whole life had been spent attaining the pinnacle of society's approval. Now he could dance with any beauty he desired, and no one would rush his intended partner away. In fact, the chaperones encouraged him to cast his glance towards their charges.

He had wanted to dance with Miss Holbrook and was glad of the opportunity, so why did the girl seem like such a child? With relief, he surrendered his partner back to her mother's care. From the glance the girl bestowed upon him, he assumed she was reluctant to leave, but more than two dances in an evening with the same partner, and he might as well send the engagement notice to the *Times*. He was not ready to select his bride from the current crop of hopeful debutantes.

Heading towards the punch bowl, he hoped to regain his first eager pleasure in the round of society's events. He surveyed the group of young girls crowding the room in their finery. Because they wore the white dresses of debutantes, they were easy to notice.

He saw pretty ones, plain ones, those who dressed with elegance, and those who did not. Girls of every shape and hue swarmed in the room like bees to a flower, displaying their charms and hoping to attract a husband. The successful girls had a group of men hovering around them. The cacophony that resulted from so much flirtatious conversation trumpeted in his ears.

Yet not one girl appeared any different to him. Despite the outward variations, each one was cut from the same inner material. The similarity disappointed him. Not one of them would ever express a thought contrary to his expressed opinion.

He sipped his punch and missed the spark in his life that Annette had ignited.

As the weeks passed through May into June, Sir Gerard still sought enjoyment from the social round, but now a desperation to find the pleasure in it seemed to dog his every activity. He went from party to rout to ball in a constant whirlwind that brought him no surcease from the pall of boredom which weighed heavier each moment on his spirit. The prosecution of Wallace brought satisfaction, but not the loss of Linton's friendship.

The respectful adulation Sir Gerard met at every social gathering wore on his equanimity. No one disagreed with any of his opinions, no matter how outrageous. Because of this continuous agreement, he had no desire to set up a mistress. Where was the excitement in that? No woman could compare to Annette. Not the giggling debutantes, the serious bluestockings, or the racy widows.

The steward continued to send reports about the estate and the renovations being done on the tenants' cottages. There was no mention of Annette, or even of her school.

It surprised him how much he longed for her expressed opinions or the sight of her capable hands at her sewing or the passionate armful he discovered when he kissed her. Still he clung to the achievement of his dream, which had taken so many years to reach. He was an admired leader of society.

So he told himself while gazing into the looking glass. He tugged at the sleeve of his coat. He was ready for another night in pursuit of pleasure.

Tonight he intended to avoid the parties that clamored throughout the city. He remembered the riotous celebration Linton and he had shared when the news of Sir Nigel's death had reached them. Then, deep play had led him into the clutches of the money-lender. Now the lack of funds was no longer a problem. He had no problems, he told himself firmly.

Sir Gerard nodded with approval. Tonight good fortune smiled upon him. He could feel it in his bones. With a final smoothing of his coat, he headed for the exclusive gaming hells on St. James's Street, where the thrill of winning hands awaited him.

Chapter Fifteen

He lost. Even as he slumped over Silver Shadow for the ride home, Sir Gerard still could not believe it. He had been so sure. His hand had been a winning hand. He knew it. But the cards had not been good enough.

Almost without being aware of it, he guided Silver Shadow through the city's crowds. On this bright May morning, everyone bustled about his business. The cry of the muffin man competed with the shrill shouts of bargaining housewives. A mixture of scents assaulted his nose, dominated by fresh-baked bread, horse, and the smoke from the coal fires that always lingered in the air. The smells turned his stomach.

Or maybe it was the late night of drinking that caused his stomach to heave and his head to whirl in this crowd. He did not know or care. He only sought to reach his home and escape under the bedcovers.

He directed Silver Shadow around a stopped wagon. "Come on, boy," he told the horse. "There is no need to be so miserable. You will recover."

His laugh sounded forced even to his own ears. Yet, there was no reason to wallow in misery. He certainly had the funds to pay off his losses. Sir Gerard shook his head and then wished he had not. He was acting as if Annette had not returned his fortune to him.

Annette.

She would not be proud of him, if she saw him now. He groaned. Why did he always live up to people's worst expectations about him? If he wanted her to admire him, this was not the path to take. He knew that.

Likely Annette would never know about this night's work. There might be the odd gossip about him in the drawing rooms of London, but he was not so important that the news would leak to Upper Brampton. Not one loss.

Yet a little voice nagged at the back of his mind, "Your uncle heard of your escapades. Why won't she?"

Only if he continuously repeated the last night's losses would word of them reach the village. Why, they might not even be reported in the society news of the *Times*.

He would never lose again.

Of course, he had claimed the same thing last evening when he sat down at the green baize table and the promise of good luck had been broken. He wondered what had happened to that promise.

Patting Silver Shadow's neck, he said, "We will keep this just between the two of us. Is that all right, boy?"

The horse tossed his head, and the upset churning within Sir Gerard began to calm. He worried over nothing. After all, he had the money to pay his gambling debts. He just was not yet accustomed to having a fortune at his disposal.

Is it yours to spend?

Sir Gerard abruptly reined in his mount. Where had that thought come from?

He glanced at the crowd eddying around him. Men and women bustled about their errands or cried out their wares. No one had stopped to speak, except perhaps to curse him as an obstacle in their paths. Amid the noise and confusion, they had not posed the question about his ownership.

Shaking his head, he nudged Silver Shadow forward. He must have drunk more than he realized. It would be best if he found his bed before he started seeing things, as well as hearing them.

What a foolish thought! Of course the money was his.

Unbidden, he remembered his tenant Tim Farmer and his new cottage. If Annette had not returned the money when she did, Sir Gerard knew he would not have been able to pay for the building and stove he had promised. As it was, the payment had been a little late, due to the paperwork involved in the transfer of possession. Now he hoped Tubbs the carpenter had not suffered by the delay. The man deserved to be paid promptly for his work. He likely had a family depending upon him.

For the first time, Sir Gerard realized using a draft on his bank would not mean he was the one paying off his debts. Only that he used the labor of others to do so. The people who worked his farms or in the other business interests he now controlled, toiled to create the money he had bet so carelessly.

Like his title, the fortune was only held in life trust. It should serve the needs of the estate. If he were honest, his gambling debts did not serve the needs of the estate. And he was being brutally honest with himself.

His lips thinned. He could not waste their hard work in such a fashion. Maybe if he had never lived in Upper Brampton, his tenants would not have names and faces, and then he could live ignoring them like the rest of society. But he had lived in the village, and thanks to Annette, he did know their names. In all justice, his work should pay his debts.

He patted Silver Shadow's neck. They were nearly at his apartments, but he did not urge the horse to a faster pace. He needed to consider where he could obtain some money of his own to pay his last gambling debts.

As before, he had no assets and no income to his name. He really only owned his clothes and his horse.

Silver Shadow was an asset.

"No!" He spoke the protest aloud.

Yet even as he cried against the prospect, he realized it was the answer. The sale of his beloved horse would bring in the money he needed.

"I will never bet again," he promised.

Still, his inner sense of justice would not allow him to misuse the fortune he had inherited. Silver Shadow must be sold, and then he would return to Upper Brampton. The need to be in that small village flamed within him. He must escape London. All the promise of the city's delights had turned to ashes when he partook of them. In truth, he had not enjoyed them. Only in Upper Brampton had he enjoyed the life he wanted. Once he finished his business in London, he would return there.

Sir Gerard directed his mount towards the horse sellers at Tattersalls. He would never gamble again. The price was too high.

The mail coach seemed destined to seek out every rut and bump on the road between London and Upper Brampton. Sir Gerard gritted his teeth as the bouncing rattled every bone in his body. Fortunately, he sat near the window and was able to grasp the strap in an effort to maintain his balance.

The burly man in the middle had nothing to hold onto. His weight shifted with every movement of the coach. Sir Gerard was taking as much of a punishment from the man's body blows as in the attack by Wallace's ruffians. There would certainly be as many bruises.

In addition to the bruising he was receiving, he had to fight off nausea. The overpowering smell of very ripe onions burned the air. The farmer's wife sitting across from him had a basketful of the vegetable on her lap. She had informed her traveling companions she was going to visit her daughter, who had three children. Apparently the onions were part of the many gifts she intended to bestow upon the mother. Or maybe it was the grandchildren. Sir Gerard really did not care to puzzle it out. Instead he concentrated on breathing through his mouth and remaining upright.

He would make no complaint about this trip.

He had to return to Upper Brampton. Now that Silver Shadow had been sold, the mail coach was the fastest way.

In an effort to ignore his surroundings, Sir Gerard tried to remember Upper Brampton. Hathaway Hall sprang into his mind as he wanted the house to be—filled with light and laughter, but the manor house was no longer the lure that reeled him in as it had last January after his uncle's death. Then he had longed to see the hall again and to know that at last it was his.

Hathaway Hall was still his. Familiarity must breed comfortable acceptance, for the house did not appeal so strongly this time. The need for something else burned within him and pulled him home. That was something he had learned. He wanted a home, not a house.

The coach hit a particularly vicious hole, sending the burly man crashing into him. Sir Gerard's breath escaped with a loud whoosh. The onions flew from their basket like rocks thrown by the village boys. One clobbered Sir Gerard's forehead.

The curses of the other passengers rang in the air as they struggled to right themselves in the jouncing vehicle. Sir Gerard would have joined their chorus, if he had not bitten his tongue. Battling to set the burly man upright, at the same time he attempted to reach the handkerchief folded in his coat's pocket. Black spots from the onion blow swam before Sir Gerard's eyes.

"Don't step on them," the farmwife shrieked. "They're gifts for my daughter. She has three little ones, too."

The woman reached down to pick up her onions rolling on the crowded floor between the passengers' feet. Her off-balance posture sent her bumping into their legs. Her foot came down heavily on his polished boot.

"Sorry, sorry," she muttered, gathering up her vegetables.

Sir Gerard smiled painfully as he pressed the handkerchief against the lump forming on his forehead. He would never forget this miserable trip. He missed Silver Shadow more than he thought possible.

But he missed Annette more.

She was the lure that drew him. London had not satisfied him because she had not been there. At every function and activity, he had missed her.

The prospect of seeing her again in Upper Brampton lifted his heart. Momentarily he forgot this wretched coach ride. Anticipation sang through his veins.

Annette. He would see Annette again.

Another vicious jolt of the vehicle reminded him of his

surroundings. With determination, he refused to allow the crowded conditions to make him downcast. He looked out the window at the passing countryside, watching the hedges and neat farms. They reminded him of the lands around Hathaway Hall—Annette's domain.

He would marry her and make it her kingdom forever. The sudden thought caused him to blink. Marry her?

But of course. In all the time he had missed her, he had not realized he loved her. Now he did. He loved her with all his heart, mind, and body.

She made his life complete, and he wanted to share the rest of it with her. He wanted to share in her dreams of the school. He wanted her to share in his building projects for Hathaway Hall's farms. Most of all, he wanted to share her bed, and maybe someday, he and she would share children.

He had to convince her, but this time, the lucky feeling surging through him like the sea against the coast would not play him false. This time he would win. All the travel inconveniences melted away.

Sir Gerard rapped on the coach's ceiling. "Get this rig moving faster!"

Annette yanked at the stubborn weed and pulled its roots free from the clinging garden soil. It felt good to attack something she could see. For so long she had struggled against the children's ignorance. Fighting to educate them was like battling an invisible enemy. She knew it existed, but very seldom did she seem to inflict any wounds upon it. Only occasionally did the spark of understanding send a student leaping ahead in his studies. Mostly it was a bitter ground warfare, as she and her pupils slugged it out over the alphabet and the basics of arithmetic.

She set the weed in her basket to be added to the compost pile later. She gazed around at her flower bed. It bloomed in a riotous green, dotted with the vivid colors of sunshine yellow, dawn pink, and periwinkle blue, providing a vibrant contrast to the gray stone front of her cottage. She could hire a boy to do such a messy chore, but doing it herself filled her with satisfaction.

When the weather turned cold again, she would be among the boys and girls again, but for now she relished her solitude. With determination, she had made her life one of fulfillment and service to others. The annuity reserved from her brief fortune would keep her and Lucille for the rest of their days.

It was enough to expect from life. She convinced herself she was content. She applied her efforts to the flower bed.

The sound of a cleared throat behind her signaled she was no longer alone. Glancing backwards, she spied the tall form of the baronet.

She sprang to her feet. "Sir Gerard! I did not realize you were there."

"Good afternoon, Miss Courtney." He strolled forward with his easy elegant air and bowed. "I appreciated the opportunity to watch you work. You are a very energetic woman."

Blushing, she became aware of how she must look. Dirt clung to her gloves, her hair was in disarray, and grass stains colored her skirt, which was not her best dress. She brushed at the clumps clinging to her gloves. "Forgive me. I am not ready to receive callers."

He grasped her hands, not minding the dirt. "I hope I am more of a friend than a caller."

"Oh," she said in a small, breathless voice.

For a moment time slowed as she gazed up into his face. The sound of a chirping bird faded away. The perfume of the flowers hung heavy in the air and mingled with the beloved scent of him. A smile quirked his lips, and his brown eyes were tender.

Recollecting herself, she blinked. "I am surprised to see you here. I had expected you to remain in London until the Season ended."

"London was not like what I had anticipated," he said. "Upper Brampton drew me back."

He did not release her hands. She was conscious of how lightly, but firmly, he held them. She could not look away from him, drinking in the sight of his face. Neither did he glance away.

"I—we—the villagers and I are certainly glad you are back." Mention of the villagers reminded her of the impropriety of standing in her front garden, where the whole world could spot her with Sir Gerard. For an instant her training took over, and she started to tug her hands free. Then she stopped, discovering she did not care what anyone else thought. After so long without him, she wanted to be near him.

"Will you come in for tea?" she asked.

"Gladly," he said.

When they turned to enter the cottage, she noticed she did not see Silver Shadow tied along the road that ran in front of her cottage. "How did you get here, Sir Gerard? I do not see either a horse or carriage."

"I walked."

Remembering his insistence that she purchase her landau, she teased him, "You would put a carriage at my disposal when I called upon you, do you expect me to return the favor?"

He laughed lightly. "But of course. You do not suppose that a man of my rank should be seen tramping through the Wiltshire countryside."

"I would think such a man would ride a horse if not in a carriage." She smiled at him, enjoying the rapport between them. "Why did you not ride Silver Shadow?"

"I sold him in London."

Stunned at the abrupt announcement, she stopped in the doorway to the parlor. "You sold Silver Shadow! But you love that horse."

For the first time, he glanced away from her gaze. "Yes, but I had to."

Concerned, she placed her hand on his arm. In a gentler tone, she asked, "What happened?"

He studied her for a moment before taking a deep breath. "I sold him to pay my gambling debts."

The words sounded ugly to her ears, but she did not shrink away from him. Even though she heard the condemning words from his own lips, she would not judge him. She did not know the whole story. But she did know she loved him. She would trust him.

"I am certain there is more to it than that. Come in, Sir Gerard, and tell me about it." Annette led the way to the parlor. "Lucille is out visiting. I will request the maid to bring in the tea tray."

"No, I do not need tea. I would prefer to speak with you without interruption."

She gestured for him to sit down, but he ignored it. The burning intensity she saw in his gaze kept her standing, too. Wasting no time on polite inanities about his trip, she asked, "Why did you sell Silver Shadow?"

"I told you to settle my gambling debts."

"So you did," she replied calmly. "But since I doubt

you went through that entire fortune in one Season, there must be more. Why did you sell your beloved horse instead of using the money at your disposal?"

The ghost of a smile curved his lips. "Always the direct approach for you, Annette."

"My information is more accurate then." She attempted to smile back at him, but it was a weak effort. Her heart quailed at what she might learn even as her mind would not let her emotions rule.

He sighed. "Unfortunately I did lose him to my gambling debts, but I did not lose the entire fortune."

She stepped forward and laid a hand lightly on his sleeve. "Please explain."

Although he ran his hand through his hair, he did not move away from her. "I went to a gambling hell expecting to emerge the big winner. Instead I lost. When the time came to pay off my debts, I realized I could not squander the labor of others in such a useless fashion solely for my pleasure. That was your influence. They were my debts. I should be the one to pay for them, so I sold Silver Shadow."

The explanation was simply told, but Annette felt a singing surge through her veins. She was glad she had not condemned him outright for gambling. Yes, he had gambled, but he had not frivolously spent his fortune.

"That was a very high cost," she said. "I am sorry your horse is gone."

"You are right. The price was too high," he told her. "I never intend to gamble again." He took her hands in his. "It was your influence that gave me the strength to do it. I admire you greatly."

Admire. Her smile became tight. Admiration was all she would ever have from her beloved. She, who knew how to stretch a farthing to do the work of a penny, could make do with admiration.

She managed to be gracious. "Thank you for the compliment."

One of his hands continued to hold one of hers while his arm went around her waist to pull her closer to him. "I learned many things while I was in London."

"So you said."

The perfumed promise of the garden seemed to have drifted through the open window, for Annette smelled the flowers and heard the bird chirping from the oak in the front yard. Sir Gerard's long body pressed against hers, and she felt dangerously secure in his arms. Despite the impropriety, she made no effort to escape. She feared to name the emotion she saw burning in his eyes, but its existence caused her to tremble with anticipation.

"One of the things I learned," he said, "was how much I missed you. I needed you in London."

"I have never been to the city," she replied breathlessly. "How could I help you?"

"Because I was lonely, Annette. Were you lonely here in Upper Brampton?"

He gave her no opportunity to reply, for his lips came down on hers. He was tender, questioning, and her body responded, *Yes, I missed you.*

She clung to him, tasting him and feeling him beneath her hands. His shoulders, his chest, and his hair that curled at the nape of his neck, she touched them all. No longer did she care that he now knew how much she loved him. She freely expressed it.

When the kiss ended, they both were breathing heavily. In his eyes, she read triumphant exultation. A smile beamed from his face.

"You did miss me," he proclaimed.

She made no effort to deny the truth. "Yes."

"Marry me, Annette. I love you."

The words struck her to stillness. She had never thought to hear either sentence from his lips, and she stared at him dumbly.

His arm tightened around her, while one hand lifted her chin. She could not look away from his face, even if she had wanted to.

"Please, I want to you to be my wife."

"But I am not the right sort of woman for a baronet," she managed to gasp out. She dared not believe she had heard him correctly.

"You are the right sort of wife for this baronet." His thumb traced a path along her cheek. "I have acted foolishly, but you have been my guiding light. I need, no, I want you with me for the rest of my life."

"You cannot possibly love me."

His smile was tender. "Do you think so little of yourself? Do you think so little of me that I would not mean my declaration?" He shook his head. "Annette, your heart is generous towards everyone but yourself. You are a woman who inspires great love."

She blinked, not daring to believe. "But I am not pretty, and the London ladies are far more sophisticated than I."

His hand smoothed back her hair, and her head rested against his touch, savoring it.

"You are beautiful." His voice was deep with emotion. "Do not compare yourself to those society women. Their polished exteriors cover only emptiness, while you have a shining spirit that beams from within." His arms tightened around her, and he held her even closer. The warmth of him echoed the fire sparking within her.

She searched his face, seeking confirmation of his words. "Do you truly want to marry me? I do not have the money anymore. It is completely yours. You do not need to marry me."

He shook his head in tender dismay. "I was never a very successful fortune hunter for money, for my true treasure is you. You are the fortune I do not want to lose."

She saw the love in his eyes and in the curve of his lips and felt it in his grasp around her waist. With a satisfied sigh, she realized life with her beloved was in her grasp. She took his face in her hands. "Yes, I will marry you. After all, someone must help you properly use that fortune."

His eyes twinkled. "I look forward to all the causes you will espouse."

Then neither one spoke again as they kissed to seal their private betrothal promises. The birds cheeping outside provided the background music as their hearts met together in mutual love and respect. They had each found their mate, and the question of the fortune's disposal had been answered. Together they would let love manage the miser's moneybags.